Dancing with Carmen

By

Gloria Tessler

L'oiseau que tu croyais surprendre battit de l'aile et s'envola ... l'amour est loin, tu peux l'attendre; tu ne l'attends plus, il est là!	The bird you hoped to catch beat its wings and flew away... love stays away, you wait and wait; when least expected, there it is!

From "Habanera", Carmen
Music composed by Georges Bizet, Libretto by Henri Meilhac
and Ludovic Halévy

authorHOUSE®

AuthorHouse™ UK Ltd.
500 Avebury Boulevard
Central Milton Keynes, MK9 2BE
www.authorhouse.co.uk
Phone: 08001974150

First published by AuthorHouse 7/1/2011

ISBN: 978-1-4389-7005-9 (sc)

This book is printed on acid-free paper.

Dedication

This book is dedicated to my mother, Regina Kien-Tessler, whose own natural story-telling and encouragement has been an eternal source of creative inspiration.

I would like to thank Diane Bramson and Julia Carbonara-Levy for their invaluable advice, and my three children Daliah, Donna and Ramon for their unfailing support.

PROLOGUE

The Legend of Carmen

In the beginning there was the dance, which moved across the waters of the deep, for the dance was everything, the soul and its devil, and the deep was the girl whose spirit was moved to dance.

At first she was just a person in the crowd, and then you saw that her deportment was of another order entirely, for she managed to generate the spirit of the dance before it even touched her body.

Gradually, the crowd divided from her, and she moved in a deeply sensuous way into a different rhythm which had no clear origin, although it seemed to incorporate Spanish-gypsy, Mayan poor-child and Arabian temptress.

After the first few moments, a handful of men left the chairs they were leaning on and felt stirred to join her, but it soon became clear that she was not inviting them in.

The closer they came the more she withdrew but less from a desire to tantalise than to liberate herself. They were not discouraged. They moved in like frisky young bulls, aroused and eager to enter her rhythm, not noticing the thread of fate woven into it, nor the peculiar sapience of the dancer, nor the fact that they were sending her into a finer dimension.

They returned to their chairs with a foolish half-smile, a smile of shame. Awkward in their own youth, they could barely sense her agelessness.

Carmen's dance was not erotic but narcissistic. It was a dance of expiation, loosening her from the bonds of place and memory.

The day faded and her hair became a blue nimbus in the light of the moon. Her muscular legs in their white stockings were the saddest and solidest thing about her. Weaving robustly beneath the short, red alpaca skirt, they suggested a fragile and painful secret, a knowledge of the world and its abuse. Her features radiated the same morbid awareness.

And so as she moved deeper into the dance, this woman of defined, contained sexuality began to change. She became a waif-woman - Prosper Merimee's peasant-Carmen as much as she had just been Georges Bizet's magisterial femme fatale.

She moved in silence, yet there was about her a sense of music, the beat of a *habañera*, the plaint of a cello in its high register, reed pipes in the Andes. There was something else: a fleeting sense of smell that roots us to memory as it freed her from her own.

Her power was not that she could lure every man in sight, but that she had no need of him. The dance thus became her own metaphor; both the secret and its discovery.

This scene of Carmen dancing in a street square near the factory where she worked, was my first sight of her. Though I grew to hate her I also loved her; for I saw her as the Lorelei of the mind's deep waters in which love and death are combined.

I do not resent you, José, for falling for her, only for not *feeling* for her.

Carmen's dance suddenly ended. The sounds returned to the night, which had its own grim heartbeat. She threw you, José, a rose of the purest blood-red, and she laughed. The laughter faded through cynicism to visceral anguish. It sent a shiver through the night street, whose heartbeat grew louder now, stronger, wiser, and the word "bitch" or "witch" - I was never sure - came from your mouth and condemned her for all time.

All down the days, from Seville to Santa Barbara, they follow her, this pied piper of sexual promise, like electrons orbiting a nucleus. At first they come as children; copycat young girls with effrontery in their voices, older women in thick stockings who remember the roll of their hips. And gradually both young and old behave as if they have discovered a more abstract, long-buried knowledge, which is the knowledge of their true selves.

Some - who long for liberation - put her in charge of their feminist hopes, for which her laughter is a symbol of both the proud and the piteous. All of those who hear her call, who sense her witchery, have caught the spirit of Carmen and will reach, if only for a moment, that plangent depth in the universe which is the eternal feminine.

Leave her to her fate, however. This is my testimony.

MICHAELA

CHAPTER ONE

Dying For Carmen

On the first day of our love I asked you whether you would think of me on the point of your death. You smiled and said what a strange question, but your face darkened with the premonition it opened between us.

"What makes you think, "you asked lightly, "that I will be the first to die?" And because I could not answer you replied that you thought I had inherited my grandmother's intuition. I felt a slight chill then. Your eyes were closed. I circled them with my fingers and felt them flutter like nervous butterflies. I could feel in you that half-formed quality of very young children when they touch your hand, still more spirit than body.

The chill deepened. I shivered and draped my coat around me, but the cold was not of this earth. The sky was still and white and a tree formed a fierce, clutching hand. Inside the white of the sky, inside the grip of the tree, I felt something dark and fearsome silently gathering.

❧

I am waiting at the prison on the morning of your last day on earth. The same heavy white sky evokes this memory of the first day, as though the intervening years are only a change of mood within a continuum.

Why am I so cold when the sun is burning its white heat down on me? I see the guards moving towards me in a leering, collusive huddle. In their eyes I am reduced from oligarchic daughter to ragdoll blonde - rape-bait. I have devalued my heritage, and upset the precise ordering of their lives.

One of the guards reaches out for the fruit I have brought for you, and as I lunge forward to grab it back, it spatters onto the ground. Grinning wildly, he catches hold of my beating fists in one grasp of his brown hand as though they are a pair of tiny birds, flapping their wings in panic.

"Pick up the fruit!" commands the one with the bayonet, poking it into my neck.

He begins to stomp around like a politician conscious that he is making a speech, then suddenly realising that he has nothing more to say. He turns to me again, full of the poison of choked wrath.

"It is José you want to see?"

I nod.

"His last supper?"

Again the poke of the bayonet in my neck.

I kneel down and retrieve the smashed guavas and pomegranates and peaches from the ground. The mushy fruit feels like blood. I ask, tonelessly, for a bag to put the fruit in.

One warder nods in the direction of the paper bag lying on the ground. The taunting one fondles my neck with his bayonet, then impales the bag on it before waving it tantalisingly in my face and throwing it away.

"You want to see José?" he repeats. The iron doors clank open revealing another enclosed space shafted by walls and a vaulted ceiling.

"Be my guest!"

Facing me is another heavy iron door, perhaps two feet away. Between the two sets of doors there is no window.

"The man in the condemned cell will enjoy eating the fruit from your hands, "he chuckles. "Why waste paper in these hard times?"

Suddenly the door through which I had entered slams shut, placing me in a damp and starless universe. Silence.

When the doors open there is no sign of the men who taunted me. I am led by two others whose eyes have no light in them down corridors smelling of urine. It is a childish, lonely smell. On each side are cells from which I am watched by countless eyes. The noise of their silence fills all the space in the world. It is the drone of trapped souls.

One of the guards pauses outside a cell door. The silence dissolves into a tinny tune on a distant transistor: "Last Train to San Fernando". Someone flushes a toilet. How blunt and distorted everything seems.

The warder opens your cell door.

I can make out your shape, huddled by the tiny window,

3

but I cannot see your face, José. Will I still recognise you? Absurd question, but it has been so long.

A chaplain appears beside me. I know him by the faint rustle of his cassock, as though it were made of some pellucid, ethereal cloth, for I cannot see his face either. There is a blur, a fuzz, today about faces.

You sit there, not bothering to look up at me. Quietly I approach and touch your hand. Already it feels empty, like a waxen glove. The chaplain folds his hands over his bible and waits, watching the warder stroke his sideburns and take out a tortilla from a brown paper bag.

When I look at you again, I see a tiger leaping in your eyes. Once you spoke of the animal waiting to claim us at our last moment - the animal which understands that birth and death meet on the same plain. We expect more. What if there is no more? No more than the broken neck, bulging eyes and the secretion of the body's last fluids at the tightening of the noose?

"I'm afraid," I say to you, with a smile, "that you will be reborn a wild animal in the next life because you did not fight for this one."

I had not wanted to say that. I had wanted to tell you how I had seen your ghost in my doorway last night, holding out a white rose for me just as you had offered a red one to Carmen.

You take my hands, cup them in yours, and ask - "How did they become so sticky?" And you begin to lick them clean, tasting the dust with the pomegranates and the peaches and the good earth and the ill will of the guard. Irreverent thoughts keep rising up, as they did with Claudius in the profanity of his prayers: have you left a will? What should I do with your clothes? For what else am I now responsible?

The tortilla-eater is busy swatting a mosquito that has entered the cell and won't stop buzzing. He slowly, stupidly lumbers towards the tiny creature which continues to evade him, throwing exultant, darting shadows on the walls. Beneath them I feel myself shrinking, José, growing colder, thinner, greyer, wishing we were both butterflies.

You stand up. And I see you suddenly age before my eyes - a sweet-dryness of ageing, like an urbane and gracious lover, whose lips pucker with dim thoughts.

The door opens. The priest, hands folded, bends to the light.

Dying for Carmen, they said.

You killed her.

So they said.

CHAPTER TWO

Street Boy For An Infanta

London, 20 years later

In the slant of this fine English rain, I am trying to remember. Once it was music, or the heat-smell of a tropical plant that did it. Now an icy wind will bring you back from the distant throb of our Latin America into this cold English climate.

I am dabbing them on, these memories, layer upon layer, like a painting. In my hands lie dead flowers smelling of excreta. I had forgotten to water them - such a glorious profusion when Pedro brought them last week - now slimy-stalked in stale brown water.

Somehow their slanted, drooping heads, like this rain, remind me of our love, which, too, came slanting, light angled through a door. That is how it was, never a straight line from you to me.

❧

It's hard to tell the exact moment when I first saw you.

You were one of the poor *campesino* children squatting in the village square, one of those who came to gape at us, not giggling furtively, as London children might do, but staring, with the old eyes of the young poor.

You see, how years later I have begun to compare - so much have my two worlds shrunk and slithered into one new skin.

I used to wait for you, after the fashionable women, the charitable-chic, the men of consequence in city suits disappeared into their hours of siesta.

And then the street became lighter, opening to the jugglers, the fortune tellers, the fruit-sellers, and all the cat-calling of the underclass, with its great, gaping wound of a smiling mouth. You came to me like a magician, offering sweets and acorns, doing handstands, pulling your mouth like a clown to kiss and then drawing back, but you never offered your friendship, never spoke a word.

I handed you a few coins. The other children instantly surrounded me, but you refused to take it. You were insulted and turned away, hiding your face. But not before I glimpsed the shut-out pride.

As for me, I was like a young *Infanta*, heavily guarded by women. I began to watch for you as I was driven home, and sometimes managed to escape once my mother and her friends started unloading their shopping, excitedly discussing the trivialities of their day.

And one day you spoke to me.

"Little girl soon to be woman," you said without tenderness. And that was all.

"He isn't interested in my feelings." I thought, surprised at my own bitterness. And I carried the anger from that day on, without knowing its weight.

It was a long time before we spoke again, though sometimes you glanced in my direction and then the audacity of your remark burned through me.

Later I saw you working the land, helping your fellow *campesinos*, energetically tilling and hoeing. It seemed to be an act totally devoid of love.

Later when the sex was in your voice, I looked at you and like a mist dissolving, I knew your heart.

I continued to accompany the other women, my mother and aunts and cousins, on their boring shopping rounds, but their excitement over small things no longer enchanted me. I felt older, superior in my secret imagination. As they talked I day-dreamed, picking over the shreds of my small memories of you, looking for clues about your feelings.

We had not spoken since you had uttered that strange phrase which had so piqued me :"Little girl soon to be woman."

Despite your slenderness, you had a manly grace and a certain density. Your movements were sharp and assured; your nose and mouth met in a soft, downward curve. The women's magazines told me what these things meant. They said your looks suggested sensuality and jealousy. To me your face showed a condign delicacy and daring.

Now the leaden sky dissolves into drifts of lighter

cloud through which a slash of blue appears. The brief sunshine illuminates the damp leaves, window-frames and the street puddles. It is as though the flow of light and laughter, rain and tears has an inevitable diurnal rhythm. I open the back door and tread gingerly into the rainbow puddle, observing it ripple away from my shoe, wave upon little wave, green, red yellow and purple. I laugh like a child.

"Suede shoes," Celia, the housekeeper, reproves me from the doorway. "You've ruined them now. Never get those water stains out."

"So what?" I smile. "I won't be needing them again."

Pedro will be here soon. He likes to see me laughing, living in the present, as he puts it. There is only the present, he keeps saying. The past is dead. He understands, for he, too, is a refugee from the past.

Poor Pedro. He comes over to shake me gently when he sees my eyes clouding over, the way you would shake up the flour in a sieve.

"You are remembering too much," he protests. "Memories make you old."

I turn away from him. I don't want to see his worried face now. How could he understand my need to lift that skin of forgetfulness, to recapture my life now, not in these sad spasms but in its entirety.

But really I first met you in a dream. I was floating beneath grey water, staring up at grey sombre buildings.

A pilot shot out of the skies, with headphones and flak jacket, talking intently to me in a language I half understood. He had your face. Then the dream changed. You were walking with a tall man's hint of a stoop, like the curve of a tree.

In my dream you told me your dreams. You laughed as you talked of desert birds pecking at you, fields coming towards you like a menacing tide. And I, reared on my grandmother's signs and wonders, tried to interpret these images as the landscape grew vivid and ominous. I saw in that dream the long, uncultivable coastal plain. I heard the ancient prayer for corn, the old communion with the source of being that eating it represented.

Rich harvests of plantation crops, coffee, sugar cane and cotton yield fortunes to the multinational companies, while our own people hunger. This is one of the things you told me, in a dream and later, much later in my awakening. Perhaps you wanted to make me feel guilty of some ancestral collusion.

CHAPTER THREE

In The Beginning Of Our Time

Let me tell you how it all happened.

That night was filled with an astounding red sky. It lit the night with shreds of vermilion and crimson, deepening to terracotta. For some reason I was pierced with the grief of those colours in the heavens. Bird shapes became soaring missiles. Edifices rose and evaporated, hands touched hands and were abandoned for other hands.

I could not sleep. I got up, dragging the night and its colours with me as though through water. In the courtyard the servants had fallen asleep among their chores like characters in "The Sleeping Beauty". The bitter sigh of the unconscious was over the house, but I felt that something in the night was waiting for me, gathering the hours of my life together.

I walked quietly back to the house, pausing at the bedroom doors to glance at my sisters, my brother, my parents, my grandmother, all in the crude exposure of sleep beneath Parisian-drapes and Flemish wall-hangings.

There was such richness and such poverty in their sleep. It made me fear the shaky balance of good and evil within human nature. I stood watching them for a long time, until it became light.

11

I quietly closed their bedroom doors, and the extraordinary day began.

I left the house at dawn and drove past the town with its broad, Latin boulevards, its city square with lazy military officers wiping traces of home-brewed guaro from their moustaches, its glassy modern parapets, towards the village of my obsession, your village, José.

It was only on leaving the glassy little town that I remembered a recurring dream.

In the dream I approached a glass tower with a key. A man was standing behind it, like a dummy in a shop window, and I smiled and waved, indicating the key. The man who was you and was not you, waved and smiled back, and I understood from his smile that the key had no lock and could open nothing.

I left the car at the village and walked to the fields where I could hear the *campesinos* working. I saw a man and a woman in the sugar plantations. The man was working non-stop cutting down the sugar cane. I heard him complain – "Two metres high and if you don't bloody cut it down in time, the locusts will eat it, damn them. And within a couple of years the land will be milked to death, yielding up its fruits to a master who cares nothing for it." He sat down, exhausted, and began to wipe the sweat off his face and take a bite or two of *torrejas* and a spoonful of fried beans. It had been raining for a few moments, as happens daily in these regions, but now a glaring, humid sun appeared, etiolating land and sky into vast light, and bringing with it the buzz of mosquitoes. He brushed one away and the Egyptian taskmaster of a foreman who was employed by the multi-national company which owned the land, sauntered by, sneering.

"If you can't take the pace, *hombre*, you shouldn't be working here."

And then the woman stepped forward purposefully, as though about to offer some dignified rebuke, but suddenly she changed her mind and began screaming abuse, raising her roughened elbow towards the foreman. They stood together - I will always remember this - an icon of doomed socialist brotherhood with their small, scared children, and the woman took another menacing step forward, towards the foreman, and again I saw that sick smile on his face, and then I saw you. The look on your face told me that the man and woman were your parents, and suddenly your mother called your name aloud: "José!" she cried and I noticed you were in army uniform. She forgot about rushing to your father's defence and suddenly we were all staring at you, in your khaki uniform, as though you had somehow come to embody the foreman's offence.

"This army. This rabble. Why, José?" I heard her yell. "To keep this bloody oligarchy in power?"

Like a blade the foreman moved between them and knocked her to the ground.

For one moment I felt you saw me. Then you calmly took out your revolver and shot the foreman. He lay without a sound, blood pouring from one eye, instantly dead.

Amid the ceaseless noise of crickets, the awful

buttermilk sky, came the click of the revolver, back in place after you had emptied the rest of the cartridges into his body. In a flash I was beside you, tugging at you, pleading with you to escape, to come with me.

You touched my face, ran your hands of glass over my features, like a man blinded by what he has done. The dream of glass - cold as your glass hands - came to me with that dim echo of warning.

Later, your mother was to tell me: "José always had his way. When I found I was pregnant with him, the youngest of twelve, and with nothing to feed the family with, I sat in a tub of hot water, desperately drinking bottles of *Secco* which we made from the sugar cane. To this day I cannot rid myself of its taste of bitter-sweet coconut, but his will to enter the world overcame everything. He looks mild but has the will of mountains."

CHAPTER FOUR

José Begins An Alien Life

"When you kill a man," you said, "you take his spirit with you wherever you go. You can never be alone again."

You burned the uniform of your enforced conscription and changed into the overalls of the murdered foreman whom you buried in the soil of the sugar plantations. One day he will grow to a great height, I observed, and his sweet revenge will engulf us.

I saw how you felt drained by the rape of land for money. Your arm was taut around my shoulders as I drove. The death of the foreman stayed in your eyes, which moved occasionally in my direction. You barely noticed, as the sun went down, that my long, distracted drive past coffee, maize and citrus farms and through the fine red dust of the hills had ended up back at the town where I lived. I barely noticed either. We were both tuned in to some new beat of the universe.

You buried your head on my shoulder. I had never seen a man cry before, certainly not one whose face crumpled like a sheet of paper and never made a sound.

"I would have done the same," I replied. "He assaulted your mother."

I hid you in a cupboard in my room while I raided my brother's wardrobe for old clothes that he would never remember having bought in the years of his New York spending spree.

Tonight, too, Alvarez, my brother, would reminisce over fast-food bars with red cupolas he mistook for churches that linked the interstate highways at every destination, and gave him an eerie sense of time-travel, always returning him to the same place.

I - planning your new identity as a friend from another town - had wanted it to be different. To meet you perhaps in an English garden where raspberries grow and the rich and poor do not fear each other. We would take such care not to squash the tiny, cellular fruit while the sun turned my hair into sheet metal and my dress into glass as we walked into some mythical film producer's countryside that was not limp with starvation.

Oh yes, how I loved these fantasies. I was only 16 years old.

I brought you in to dinner, your hair brushed and gleaming. Your smooth neck and slight hunching of shoulders had the tension of a toreador. I could see the hard hunger in your eyes that was so foreign to us. Alvarez gave you a peculiar glance or two before he returned to his steak, doubled up like a hunter over his prey. Otherwise my family who were bred to the low voices of good table manners, did not turn a hair. With perfect smiles and outstretched hands, they welcomed you. Only my grandmother, meek as a ghost in the years of her decay, brushed past me and placed a soft hand on my shoulder, as though she understood that I had come into a time of love.

She looked at you piercingly and remarked:

"In the degenerate soil of our times, fear and ambition are hardy weeds and true love will not flower easily."

Then she sat down as though she had never uttered a word, inclined her head in a moment's prayer for what she was about to receive and began to eat.

Before my grandfather had died, the two had lived in a small villa attached to our grand one; their corridors did not echo as ours did. They lived simply, with a few batik wall hangings she had made as a young girl, an artistic talent, she declared, that I had inherited.

He liked to bash out the Bach Brandenberg concertos on an organ he had rescued from the church after the politically-minded priest fled persecution and the people no longer dared seek refuge in places of sanctity.

There was a red chalk step leading up to their house, that I liked to touch and smooth over, as a child, feeling the chalky deposits that rubbed off on my hand. It had the colour and texture old age. Then my grandfather died, shrunk to the size of a child on the bed, and quite unable to move, apart from the working of his tiny, crumpled mouth on the cup with which I would try, in his final days, to feed him pepper soup to revive him.

The silence of his terminal illness helped me grow used to the deeper silence of their bedroom after he had passed away and beyond this silence, another, the silence of things hushed up. In the wake following my grandfather's death, many people came in black coats and hats to pay respects. They came with bowed heads and courteous manners, but before long they were exchanging business cards and talking of what's on Broadway, raising their voices and sometimes laughing out aloud.

Time heals, people told me. It didn't, because I could never forget the wasted face on the pillow which had mysteriously disappeared with such absurd dignity, never to be seen again. What happened instead, was something strange for a young person. I felt that life had loosened its grip on me, disconnecting me from my past and offering me freedom from both pain and pleasure.

Sometimes when I visited my grandmother she offered me Turkish coffee and would then up-end the cup into the saucer and pick out from its dark, sediment the symbols of my future. The black squiggle which she could see was a woman, not a man, which was myself, and the one tall, unbending shape which was a man - the only real man - for which she declared life prepared me.

When eventually the family decided grandmother should move in with us, they closed up the villa with the red, chalk step, and forced upon her their solid corporate identity. It worked in one way: a sad, slow shuffle deadened her movements, and in her clothes you could smell the sickly-stuffy odour of physical decline.

Yet in her decline I also saw her growth. "Aren't you scared of getting old, grandma?" I used to say. She sighed.

"A human being occupies many bodies in the course of a lifetime, but most people are fools and believe they have only one. In the same way they can't see old age in the young nor youth in the old."

Her words made no sense to me at the time, but I nodded, intrigued and wanting to believe, hoping that enlightenment would one day follow.

Usually at dinner time, the family would discuss the day's events. My brother, Alvarez, would talk about New York, my mother would complain about the domestic staff. But tonight, all you could hear was the clatter of cutlery on the plates. And then my younger sister, Alma, who had inherited my grandfather's musical talent and played both cello and piano, laughed out aloud. As she became more involved with her music, she grew less and less communicative, until finally she stopped talking altogether.

But sometimes - as now - she would stare at something for a long time and begin to laugh: it was a laugh of uncanny perception that made me shiver. She stared at you, and then at me, and it came to me that, looking into her strange, perceptive eyes, you did not see my sister but the foreman you had just killed.

Suddenly you stood up and coughed. " Please excuse me. Don't think me rude but – "

"He's had a bad day and would like to go to bed," I said for him.

"No, don't speak for him, Michaela," my father said. "Sit down, young man. I want to talk to you, to get to know you better. As for your day, I am sure you wouldn't exchange it with mine. I've lost a fortune in shares due to a corrupt broker, I've had to sack three employees and my back is so bad that soon I shall be walking with a stoop, and not one of those charlatans that call themselves doctors, will do anything but snicker behind my back that even money can't buy health."

The telephone rang. My father answered it with a sharp "Yes", and a "No", replaced the receiver and began to explain his own fears: fear of the government and his fellow oligarchs whom he couldn't trust, fear of the left wing opposition movement; fear of the escalating murder rate, for nearly every day someone went mad and began shooting people at random.

"When these inexplicable murders take place, people are actually relieved that at least something has happened to break the tension. Can you believe that? But I'll tell you something else: you can sense from the mood on the streets during the following days, that the killers acted less from political conviction than from an eruption of impossible and irreconcilable feelings. These feelings have entered them like a cancer. It's not their fault. They're always promising themselves a new world that can never be theirs. Silly dreamers!"

Whenever one of these random murders occurred, without apparent motive, without any attempt at explanation, the international journalists filled the coffee shops and bars of the Glass Houses, and peered up blankly from above their notepads and tape recorders and watched us, the so-called privileged ones, pass by. Sometimes the photographers would snap us women as we passed pausing to adjust a shoe strap or a gold earring, and then we would appear in the foreign papers the next day juxtaposed against the face of some poor and dirty child to illustrate an article condemning the divisions of rich and poor in our society. And yet, I thought, they were the worst hypocrites of all, because of the celebrity culture their stories and pictures bred. And like all epidemics, it spread to us, too.

The women whose faces had been chosen were elated, and preened and gossiped together about "instant stardom", and then there was laughter and speculation in the Glass Houses about going to Hollywood or becoming a supermodel, while the newspapers and magazines were passed between them. It was my grandmother who understood the deeper message. "The world is waiting for civil war," she remarked. "If the media could bring it on without us, they would."

But we tended to dismiss her doom-laden predictions. And when I opened a European magazine to see my own face staring back at me it went to my head, too. I took in the jewellery, the hairdo, the designer dress, and up till then I saw nothing else.

My mother stood up suddenly and went over to the magazine rack, and as if she had read my mind, came over to us with a knowing smile and placed the journal with my face on the cover on the table between us. She said nothing but continued to stand there, wearing that superior smile, and we both read the political message in the gesture.

You sat listening to my father's unending tirade, your eyes on the face on the front cover which in your eyes I saw no longer belonged to me, until your head drooped, and my father grumpily relented. "Take him to his room, Michaela," he said.

CHAPTER FIVE

The Moulding Of A Lover

A false identity, an alien life-style. Tailors came with cloth and tape-measures. They had obsequious faces. We spent days in shops. You grew a neat moustache, cut and greased back your curly hair.

Ownership came easily to me: I had seen others bought and sold, distorted by new wealth. Even my elder sister's husband, who had not come from one of the leading families, had to undergo a similar process, and he was no refugee from police or poverty.

In your case I was less cynical. I thought in terms of transformation, not transaction. I hoped that luxury would soften the toughness around your mouth, the distant sadness of your eyes. But I knew that you yearned for the family abandoned in the village and I feared that if the right moment came, you would leave me and return there without a backward glance.

Much later I admitted to you that I had sent bribes down to quieten the local industrialists in your village and that I had secretly opened a bank account to help your family. When you learned this you became both relieved and furious. Nobody, neither the bank, nor even the industrialists, knew the true source of this munificence, I reassured you. Wealth can make you invisible if you want. It made me feel you as clay in my hands, moulding you into the man I wanted. Your otherness, your emotional involvement with your family was surely turning your mind into the clay I needed.

You turned and posed for the fitting. Most patiently. Clay on the potter's wheel.

"Is that a comfortable length, sir - and do the shoulders look too broad - what do you think?" The fitter, plaintively, on his knees, tape-measure in mouth and pins in his left hand, looked to me for assurance. I would nod my assent or point out a fault. Your mind was elsewhere: your face tense with these other thoughts.

"My father will take you into business with him, you'll soon get the hang of it," I said.

You stared through me.

"What the hell do I know about business?"

"No cheap shirts, Michaela," My father insisted. "Only the finest cotton; it must crisp in your hand and crackle and crinkle when ready for the iron: like a true aristocrat it must command its wearer's respect. Never be tempted by a man-made substitute, for that suggests the practical needs of the shirt have dominion over the man."

From where I stood I could see the taut curve of your collar, as you turned towards me for approval. I watched you smooth down the new cloth of the suit with an almost imperceptible air of respect as you gazed at yourself in the mirror. But then it faded, and I could see the expression on your face was that of a man who does not own his own life.

Sometimes, during these long tailoring sessions I would order the driver to drive around once, twice, even three times more - just so that I could keep you in my dream a little longer, because as soon as you saw me you would leap to your feet and all I could think of was my father snipping you into shape like a paper doll.

But then you gazed at me with such joy - raising your hands as though to fondle my hair, and then letting them fall back, with a sigh, because you dared not. I couldn't imagine we could ever become lovers.

But your sadness was a door opening on to an extended world. A world of fields and rivers of knowledge and experience, colours and odours deeper and more intense than I had ever known. When the door closed I felt more the prisoner than you. Sometimes the despair I felt was so great that all I could do was to grip the hands that would not touch me.

"This is not the way, Michaela," you said. "There are so many obstacles. Be realistic."

"It's the way it is," I replied, when I found words. Some words. Not the right ones. It sounded so stubborn. "And in any case, what other way? Well? Do you have another way?"

I paid the bill and we left the wine bar, and suddenly the world of glass and expensive shops melted into the poorer streets where windows were smashed and boarded, where billboards were curling down and the walls full of graffiti, where the beggars and amputees lay on the ground, some in cardboard boxes. They smelled of rot and gangrene.

Old women with arthritic fingers and the eyes of witches beckoned us with candy, reminding me of the evil crone who tried her best to kill the Sleeping Beauty.

We passed among shouting newspaper vendors, mothers and babies, filthy and dishevelled as they lay in the streets, holding out their hands for money. I began to realise that the evil I sensed was only a passing cloud that hovered over their broken spirits, and that the eyes I shuddered from contained the bitter wisdom of stillness.

Then I shuddered for another reason. Perhaps the evil was ours. I was ashamed.

I saw some of my cousins dispensing charity among the children without even a pause in their conversation, while a few drunken *campesinos* emerged from mud-huts, bumping into the lottery ticket sellers and waving machetes into the air which was stale with hopelessness.

A whole space, a chasm, had opened out between my life and yours. Between my life then and now.

The poor street before me was unrecognisable. Although I had been here before, I could not remember this vastness. It was a market place that opened out to fill the world. I became terribly afraid. If this place filled the world, how would I ever get out of it! The cosy world in which I had grown up became a mirage. But in the next instant the unremitting poverty of the market place became a ball of clay into which all the poor people in the street with all their colour and all their clamour were being squeezed - eyes, noses, mouths, all screaming and groaning, out of existence.

I stood staring into empty space, ashamed of my fullness in their emptiness.

Then you said, "It is impossible to reach the worlds you want, that you think I represent, without first understanding this place."

You did not come home that night and I did not sleep.

CHAPTER SIX

A Saint And A Signal

And so finally the smart suits did not triumph over impoverished humanity. I began working with you in the streets, bringing fresh water to the sick, bringing the gangrenous and the leprous into our courtyards. I tore up my fine clothes and made tourniquets out of them. I became the subject of much gossip. At first it was decided I was either mad or a saint.

But because of my family's powerful name, people became superstitious and began to imagine the craziest, most unthinkable things. It was even hinted that, like Venus, I had not been born naturally, but emerged fully grown from an enormous crater caused by a meteorite in the middle of the desert.

It was said that I communed with extra-terrestrials who descended at night from the spirits of long-extinct volcanoes. People argued among themselves as to whether all this was a good or a bad omen.

These whispers became such a powerful force that even my mother began to believe them, forgetting the pains of child-birth whose torments she had handed down to her daughters with more passion than love, lest Eve's duplicity should ever be forgotten. She began to look at me with questioning eyes.

My sister, who rarely spoke, understood the power of self-hypnosis better than any of us, and laughed like a hyena every time I entered the room. Even my father, who had little time for any speculation beyond stock exchange deals, shrugged and called it no bad thing. Such rumours would only increase respect for the family, he declared.

In any case, my family had spies. Eyes everywhere. You did not know the kind-hearted friend from the skulking enemy. I thought of places where we could be ourselves, free to love.

I imagined what it would be like to make love to you. Your distance was my penance. It excited and scared me to hear your breathing in the next bedroom from mine like the ebb and flow of the sea. I used to wait for your breathing to cease so that I would know you were dead and I was free from you.

In that waiting period when each of us was so intensely aware of each other, divided by a closed door we dared not open, it became a time of signals. I was already awake to hear the dawn rustle of your sheets as you turned over and got out of bed. I learned to read the signals. Two coughs in the morning meant that you wanted to wake me. A decisive step towards the bathroom - that you thought the time for messing around was over. A calm retreat into the bathroom and the gentle closing of the door before you turned on the shower - that you had decided to go more carefully with me. The impatient brushing of your teeth - that you could hardly bear your own inaction. Lying in bed late, without tossing or deep breathing meant that you were in acute anguish over what to do with me. And best of all the soft but insistent whisper of my name.

You paused for a second outside my door each morning before going downstairs. I knew your longing as I knew the fate lines on my own hand, and still I wanted confirmation of it. All this light and sound reminded me of two prisoners in adjoining cells, who commune but never meet. This helped me cope with the emptiness of the time when nothing moved between us, when we were like two fields lying fallow.

Our conversation over breakfast with the rest of the family was shallow and purposeless, subordinated to the tinkle of plates and cutlery, punctuated by those tiresome questions. I poked at the fruit, remembering how a servant at our table used to take an orange from me and peel it without my asking her, poking her finger into the centre, until the juice ran like a moat around the plate. It made me nearly sick to watch her, but to protest would have meant her sudden removal - to where? A prison for offending servants? Perhaps summary execution? Better to stay silent.

Years later, it was still the same. Nobody ever raised a voice or lost their temper at our table. No individual energy was ever acknowledged. No laughter or tenuous expression to enable us to know ourselves and our interaction with each other.

The silence between us caused by the family blockade intensified.

Sometimes before getting up or sitting down at the table, we touched. Backs of hands. Mouth on hair.

So nobody noticed. As if in the real world such things never happened. Don't touch. Don't walk on the grass. Only in the childish world of play, of make-believe, this was allowed. So - we were children still. We could not help touching. It was like a magnetic force and you can't argue with a magnetic force.

Once in the night you called out - not whispered - my name.

I was scared of becoming your lover.

As I lay there frightened I heard my sister playing the piano. She who never spoke began to sing, in a deep, mysterious voice. It was the sad growing-away song of a young man's love for his mother who is urging him to marry the shy and blushing girl next door.

I could feel your sobs.

CHAPTER SEVEN

José's Rebellion

I lie in bed, looking down at myself naked. The flat belly, between two breasts each slightly tilted away. In this position I see their small fullness. Between them I am a path leading down to a ravine. My landscape is one colour. Softer than a desert this peach flesh, but a desert still. Dotted down below with tufted scrub where the land parts.

There are possibilities in a desert. Everything is open.

There is no youth, there is no age.

I think of you lying next door and think of my body as a passive landscape waiting to be discovered. But still, it is only a body. Then I see the toes sticking up from my feet and there is an ending. To pleasure. To life. Even before it has begun. My upturned toes, so virginal, unpainted shells of nails - like molluscs with nothing of sex or allure on them - tell me that I am also dead. I am a corpse as much as a living woman.

Next door I hear you sigh.

You have taken to drink. You begin coming home late, later, and sometimes not at all. When you do come home quietly closing the door, in the late, sour dawning of guilt, I am repelled. I can smell it on your body even through the door.

And yet I am stirred by this gingery, visceral smell. A wild child rampaging. It attracts and repels. Better to lie here still and just imagine.

One night I heard you coming up the stairs, stumbling and coughing. I burst out of my room to see you looking up at me. In your stupor you were quite unable to handle the weight and gravity of your own body. You stood there, swaying, your eyes, which held me for an instant, going, fading, paling away into some other place I had never seen in you. The smell of whisky was on your breath, on your clothes. You exhaled deeply and moved on up towards me with precarious control, moving like a man in a fog who believes himself to be the only solid factor in the universe.

You seemed large and strangely unphysical, as though you were reaching out for something beyond your grasp. I had never seen your eyes so pale. So vacant. Then at the top of the stairs where I stood, you bowed in a cynical way, opened your door, took off your coat and threw it on the bed.

"I've waited long enough."

"Not drunk, José," I said. You held on to the doorknob and the vacuous expression came and went, came and went.

"This bloody shit of your family."

"No. That's not the reason. "I held myself tightly together and closed my eyes. The fear was raging again. "I need to know", I muttered involuntarily.

"What do you need to know? There's nothing to know.

Do you want it or don't you?"

Suddenly I saw how deceitful, how self-deceiving all our patience had been. I saw how like war love is. Trysting, warring, taking sides, winning, losing. So I smiled and lowered my eyes and said: "Perhaps I need an induction course. A lexicon or something. I'm so inexperienced, José."

"Do you really want to read a book about it?"

I said nothing, so you continued with a brutal sarcasm:

"Do you want to play games for the next five years? Games of hide and seek in a big house where you can always get away?"

You sat down onto the bed and took off your shoes.

You started muttering how it would be no use, for my father would throw you out of the house what with my being a daughter of the oligarchy, which made it sound like being the daughter of the Grand Inquisitor, which I suppose for you it was.

"And what does he want of me, anyway, your father?" he asked. "What does he think I'm doing here?"

Other things you said. Words I had read about in porn magazines, giggled over with my girlfriends.

You came close and said you wanted to fuck me; you said that a man and woman were not all spirit but animals from the waist down that wanted to control and destroy, brains, heart, didn't come into it, then you said that a man must not become an animal, and that death was part of love and that every love-making, every time a man fucked a woman there was death between them, too, because you died, you both died and when that happened you were complete again, until the next fracture, the next healing love-death. I said, be careful, we'll be overheard, but you said fuck them too, and then I touched your arm to silence you.

Now your voice softened and came to me from a distance of passion but your words and meaning were insistent, and you said that everything else but what you said now, in the truth of inebriation, was bullshit, life, this bloody country and the suffering of the masses was all bullshit, too, and all to do with power, someone else's power over you, and every civil war, every battle against a foreign dictator, every act of terrorism was the same thing, and you had to smile and pretend because if you didn't you were finished, and then I said, how can you be so stupid, and that those words of yours sound like envy, because it was easy to envy the rich and say they were corrupt when actually it was poverty that was corrupt because it led to jealousy, and you said yes, that was right, both things were right, or rather wrong, but things could change, you had to believe in the possibilities of change, that you were going to change the world yourself, and become powerful and fight it, but my father couldn't have that and it wasn't right, wasn't fair either, so goodnight, sweet princess, for you must marry into your own class and close your eyes and your ears so nothing like this will ever touch you again. Nothing so coarse as the hairy wart of truth, you said. And then you said, forgive these ravings of a drunk and disappointed man. I'll be alright in the morning. Just give me black coffee for my hangover if you see me at breakfast.

I said that if you felt you had such important work to do in the country, then you must stay sober. Control your impulses.

"Stupid girl, I'm drunk because of you," you answered.

"You frighten me," I said. You folded my hands in yours and kissed them and looked closely into my eyes in that meaningful way of people who are pissed out of their minds.

"No," you said. "I don't frighten you. I make you confront your own fears."

Then you drew back and began pointing your finger as though the gesture might conceal the unsteadiness of your body. I glanced into the hallway to make sure we hadn't wakened anybody.

"We have to be quiet now," you whispered loudly, "and behave like good children so the adults won't notice our badness, our bawdiness, our lust."

I helped you back into your room.

Your drunkenness was a will to fragmentation. It was like splintered imagination; tiny glassy shards of thought thrown out in all directions, compulsive and threatening. Once you were sober I doubted that they could be put back together again.

I sat up on my bed all night, watching the eerie shape of the dresser in the dark, a solid weight of rosewood, with its glint of silver brushes and perfume bottles.

I practised a game I used to play on my own as a child. If you squeezed your eyes nearly shut then the furniture that looked so awesome in the night didn't exist. You could pass through it into somewhere else. Like Narnia.

You had come to me with a sense of somewhere else: the somewhere else was exciting. It had a feeling of ascent. And I pushed you away. I was always pushing you away.

And yet - perhaps I was mistaken. A musty smell of loneliness had come from your room when I followed you in. The kind of smell old people have. People who feel unwanted and unloved. It's on their clothes, their coats hanging on doors. It's in their hair. It was in your hair, too. The room was full of things you had collected that told me where you had been. Empty nothing places. Stubbed out cigarettes, paper napkins from burger or tapas stalls, in a tidy pile as though they might be worth keeping for a rainy day. Tins of food and beer lying among scattered underwear. A heap of shop bills. Things that suggested you didn't quite trust us. The room had a ransacked air. Like the mess of an open handbag. A disgorged feeling.

I had deluded myself. Even as we worked among the poor, our relationship was fragile and cursory.

At breakfast the next morning I deliberately provoked you.

"I heard you come in late last night, José," I said as though nothing had taken place between us." Where were you?"

You looked up over the top of your newspaper, trying not to show your surprise.

You replied that you had been playing cards in a local bar and having hit a winning streak you could not leave.

"A drunk and now a gambler?" I murmured. My father had not heard. He was involved in an impatient telephone conversation with someone. His life was spent on the phone.

You picked up your paper again and shook out its crease and there was a pucker about your mouth, a quiver of victory, which pleased me. My father went out of the room grumbling that an associate had cheated him and would surely be made to suffer for it, and you turned around to watch him go then suddenly thrust the newspaper down, stood up and gripped the table so hard I wondered if you were not still drunk.

You placed your hands on my shoulders.

"Little girl with college education and money to spend. Look around you. Your empire is crumbling. Your home is a lavish monastery. Look at the streets. The masses are growing. Look out of your own window. The beggars and the blind men are coming nearer. They are the meek. They shall inherit. But not quietly. The wars of the dispossessed are coming. Where will you hide? They will pluck you out, they will pick your brain from your head, they will smash you to pieces. Your days of sweet power are numbered. And what will you do? You will fly to Paris and buy some new clothes."

I was silent for a long time. Then I shook your hands off my shoulders.

CHAPTER EIGHT

Carmen

My parents had eyes everywhere. At night servants were made to patrol our house. You could hear them; clip-clop of soft shoes on the marble. A ghost-walk. The family lived and slept in fear. Of what? Something untoward will happen, was all my parents would say. That was their word. Untoward. I imagined armed robbery, thieves in the night, although the gates were high and the walls electrified. They did not say they were afraid of subversives, or the Agents of Death, as the peoples' militia, were called.

They did not say they were afraid of children who had turned to crime or terrorism to feed their drug addiction.

I concluded they were afraid of themselves.

I, too, did not want to think of the ravaged face at the window.

Nevertheless it was a miracle that you got past the patrol on those nights when you came home drunk. Perhaps the servants heard an echo of themselves within you for they must have known. They said nothing. But they lowered their eyes when I passed.

Mostly I remained in my room clutching my ears to

block out the piteous sounds you made. Sometimes I heard you groan. I was afraid you might fall down the stairs, hurt yourself, hit your head, go into a coma. The drink was the long river that flowed between us, heavy and polluted with false hope.

❧

After my grandfather died I used to go up to their house, past the little red step and lie on his bed. They had two beds, my grandparents. I tried to sense him within myself. The way he lay there, like one of those shrunken heads that tribesmen would bring home as trophies, his hair a wispy white trail on the pillow.

I could remember what he had been like. He used to sing snatches of opera, Gershwin, or Cole Porter. I could no longer catch his face - that came only in sudden strobes of inner light - but his voice was easier. It was easier to snatch his personality through the remembered cadences of his voice. At the bottom pitch of this melodious voice there was a deep giggle - especially when he forgot the words and tried to make them up.

I heard the tunes in my head again. When the forgotten words wouldn't come, I tried to make them up as he had done. It didn't sound quite right.

The years never smoothed out the wrinkles of these songs. No other music filled the silence of his passing. He had laughter and music, which had passed with him, and now a heavy torpor filled the house.

When I thought of the songs his death became a deep

stain that started to spread, blotting out the place I had come from. I wanted to feel what death was like. If I saw everything in place here, as it was when he died, then surely I was seeing it with his eyes and dying there with him. Within him. That way death could be lived as eternal life.

That way consciousness could conjoin. And it would be happy. It would sing.

I lay there, head lolling to one side, as I had last seen him, and then I caught sight of my face in the mirror of the walnut dresser. My face, the face of a little girl, not a shrunken corpse.

After that I never went back there any more. The house was boarded up so that not even the servants could go in. But they couldn't take away my memory of it - the old European walnut furniture bathed in the phosphorescent sun at noon. I imagined it all held together in a black cobweb, like in a Dracula film, past webbed to present.

After he died my mother refused to get up from her bed for a month.

It made me sad. My father was gentle with her at first but in the end he lost patience. He started bringing home prostitutes. He tried to shame my mother out of the lassitude of grief. The women were drunk and gaudy. My mother took the hint and began putting bits and pieces of herself back together again. I say bits and pieces because that's what they were. They never became whole, the whole I had known before. It was like trying to mend a smashed vase. You could always see the glued edges. The fine cracks were like tiny burst blood vessels.

Sometimes in her room she would take to drink.

I used to hear words from the kitchen staff as they poured dough into tins, as they sharpened knives to cut meat. Money can buy. Said the servants. Over and over again. Money can buy.

I loitered in the kitchen and ran my fingers around the inner rim of the cake tin and licked them.

❧

"Can't we go away somewhere?" I said.

"Let's take the car and drive off. Somewhere. Anywhere," you said. I liked this urgency about you when you were sober. In the countryside the trees waltzed together like lovers as we defied the speed limit.

I put on the car stereo. I turned it off.

"Do you sing, José?" I asked you. "I have never heard you sing. My grandfather used to sing."

"What did he sing?"

"I can't remember what they were or what they were called. I just remember the songs, the tunes."

"Sing them to me".

"No."

"Why?"

"It's not the same."

You had a cold that day. I remember. Because it changed you; the cold made you warm, throaty and husky; made me want to cling tightly to you for warmth. It also deepened your voice and made you different. Made me know you with different sounds.

We came to another town. Not a large one. A little local industry. A tobacco factory. People milled into a large square, idly curious. This expensive shiny red car. I regretted not having parked it further back. It drew attention, made people too curious.

What it was to experience flight. Hand in hand with you as we walked in the unknown town. You coughed a little and blew your nose. The handkerchief was white with blue edging, and your initials, which I'd had sewn into it. Everything about you was mine, I felt that day. Even your cold. I didn't want to say that to you, but I wished that I could have done.

But then the ecstasy of escape faded into a feeling of being chased, hunted down. I can hardly explain why this day a terrible fear bore down on me.

But I tried to quell the fear because I became aware of something magical about this town. It was run-down, of course, you could not get away from the poverty, but there was something else here, a stirring of joy in the milling of the crowd around the factory, young men waiting for girls. A bell rang. I noticed it the way you notice such things with such intensity in a strange place.

And then a troop of girls poured out, some smoking, some humming, brightly dressed in scarves and colourful skirts. They loosened their hair from the bandannas of their working day and let it flow down to their shoulders. There was a sense of arousal, of the anticipation of sex.

The men began singing in little groups, linking arms. Some got down on their knees and began playing troubadour to the girls with imaginary guitars. One or two had real guitars and serenaded them. With giggling and forgetfulness, stopping in mid-song and repeating the phrases over and over again to get them right.

I saw some soldiers approach and tried to draw you behind me, to shield you, as you were wanted for desertion and murder, but the soldiers had an off-duty air and were already joining the throng, fondling and touching the girls, and being encouraged or repulsed by them. One girl teased a soldier and then slapped his face as his hand touched her breast.

Beneath the playfulness of the scene there was a certain pathos about the women in their workaday entry into a brief, fragrant mood.

You noticed it. You said rather pointedly:

"Even though they are poor and can barely subsist on their wages, they know how to live."

Suddenly there was silence. A low hum that sounded like a fate theme. The crowd ebbed with one soul to the side of the factory wall. A young girl dressed in red and black was slowly and with great dignity, walking down the outer stairs.

The girl yawned and extended her strong and slender arms upwards, taking a scarf from her head and holding it taut above her head. She made no acknowledgement to the waiting crowd. She stood there for a moment and then lowered her eyes and saw them. She cast her eyes over them all and without smiling continued to descend the stairs, moving like a dancer. Languid, then sharper, as though the air was solid rock from which she was carving her likeness.

Then her voice took over. It was a *habañera*, a song I had never heard before but I have never forgotten it, and the place in which she sang it has become associated with that tune.

It cast a spell. Now Carmen, for that was her name, began weaving a web into which she gathered the crowd. Men and women alike. Her sharp little face had a tigerish intensity. Black eyes, clearly focused, showing an extreme intelligence. A small straight nose. Full red lips. I wondered at her rags, given these talents. Such a person could surely choose her life, I thought.

But her face kept changing. Sometimes you saw a coltish sensitivity. Sometimes a brutal harshness.

The dance over, she moved like an ordinary woman between her admirers, teasing, flicking a nose, gracing a cheekbone with one long hand. All gestures of denial. She could have been choosing vegetables at a market.

And then she saw you. She threw you a rose.

You stood up, swore, and brushed it away.

CHAPTER NINE

Hungry Faces

Is this all?

What else was there?

Something I have forgotten, or buried as a dog buries his bone. A bone of contention between us.

Something about your face, her face, as you looked at each other.

I don't know what it was. Perhaps it will come back.

I remember that she threw you a rose and you said fuck you and chucked it away. And the name Carmen was a hum in the air and you said let's go before she draws too much attention to me, but you were different afterwards, inside yourself somehow, and the smell of her was all over you as though you had kissed, or at least touched, been touched by her.

I'm not jealous, I said afterwards. I don't get jealous. Did I say this? I'm not sure. Why did I say it? So stupid. Confession strips you bare. Surrenders power. And what did she have to offer, after all? I could offer you a new life, new hope. She was just a poor gypsy girl. I could snuff her out if I wanted. Just like that. Like a puff of cigarette smoke.

I remember nothing of the journey home.

If there is something more, it will come back to me. Give me time.

❧

Today in the streets for the first time I touched the face of a little girl who was staring at me. I had brought food for the street children from my kitchen. This time I had made it myself. You told me that was important.

I had never touched her before. Or any of them. The others, as usual, hovered silently, like sparrows looking for bread. They never spoke. Sometimes I gave them food, other times I just threw them coins. I threw the money up in the air for fun to see the golden round shapes flutter in the air, catching the light, falling into the bronzed hands of the hungry children. Some laughed as they scrambled to catch them. When they laughed they were children playing a game. Not beggars. Mostly they resembled dying flies in the damp heat of the summer. They were often too weak to beg, or even to reach for the money. You didn't touch them. They carried germs said my mother. She would have said vermin but something stopped her.

This child's eyes were like those of an animal. It bothered me that I could not see her in human terms. Yet her eyes also reminded me of something I had lost a long time ago.

Behind the child was a tree with a bird. Behind them was a wall and behind the wall was a beautiful garden I used to play in. The deep perfume of the summer came from the garden. At that moment I wanted to forget the child and what she represented and lose myself in the tree and the bird. But when I looked at them I couldn't see them properly because what came up between them were words people used to describe them. The adjectives were not simply clichés but actually stopped you seeing them. They also stunted their growth.

I wanted to study the tree and the bird without the silly, limiting words getting in the way. The tree grew eyes and protuberances of its own old flesh, the layers of skin showed its age and the white of the bark was like white hair. It had passed through the centuries in the stillness of its own body as we shall never do. How many murders, how many courtly dances had it witnessed? I imagined a sarabande taking place on the lawn before the tree, I could hear the swish of capes against breeches, and the sigh of crinolines as the ladies curtseyed. I envied the tree what it had seen and I envied it for its patience. I saw the patience in its roots, and I saw the pain in its branches. Some of the leaves were eyes and others were hands. Each one was full with expression.

I wanted to understand. I wanted to be filled with hope.

Then I saw the child staring at me. I kissed her and picked her up onto my shoulders so that she could see the garden just behind the streets of her impoverishment. She was paper thin. She offered no resistance.

But the garden and the street were the same to her. I understood that in my fantasy about the tree I had for a moment been her eyes. But now the spell was broken.

I wanted a child so that he or she would not suffer this blindness. I wanted this child because she was close to you. You came from her. A fierce, dark child who was of the people. I feared then that I would never have your child, José.

Suddenly the streets felt cold, strange and dangerous.

In the unquestioned politeness of most powerful families, a warm welcome was always extended to their children's friends. My parents could not have imagined I might be harbouring an army deserter, no matter how odd your behaviour. But of course you were safe only as long as you stayed under our roof and I tried not to see how restless this made you to leave.

I watched your face as you listened to my father's endless business speculations on the telephone. He spoke to exporters, bankers, foreign associates, his face reddening, his voice rising. He was always hot with ideas, and bad temper. No matter how well we lived, he could never enjoy it, for he was too busy wheeling and dealing on some other plane, foreign to me, inhabited by financiers, investment consultants and foreign powers.

"I'm glad I deserted from the army," you told me. "I was forced to enlist, but at least I thought it would offer some security to my family. Now I have heard your father's conversations with agricultural judges and coffee barons, I have seen the army's true corruption and it confirms only too clearly what I already knew - that our people are slaves to a land they will never own."

While I understood this analysis, it was hard to hear my family so demonised.

My father put down the phone and stared narrowly into space.

"Señor," you said politely. "Is it right, do you think, that two per cent of the population should control 60 per cent of the land? And is it right that most of the rural population has enough work for only one third of the year?"

My father put down his glass of whisky and gave you a shrewd glance. Then he looked at me as though he suddenly understood everything.

"Sixty percent of the land you say? If the insurgents take over 100 percent of the land will be covered in blood. Perhaps you like this statistic better? "

He closed his newspaper and added with calm malevolence:

"Is this the reason you have accepted my hospitality? To throw it in my face?"

He gave us both a dark look and picked up the phone again.

From that day on I sensed more national guardsmen prowling the streets on the lookout for subversives. In my obsession I felt that every eye was trained on you. But I was afraid to reveal my fears to you.

I sat in my room alone, staring at the wallpaper until its patterns assumed bitter shapes. I moved through these shapes, which became a series of kaleidoscopic corridors leading me in. Devils' heads grinned at me and turned into skulls which began to disintegrate before my eyes. Their eyes became one eye which became the noose of the hangman's rope. The rope was around your neck but the next moment it became a serpent which grew hands and legs and crawled painfully on its belly.

I heard a voice which said: "Now I have restored the serpent to its first innocence". Mountains rose up beside you as you ran away from the serpent, so that your path narrowed and then plunged into a ravine. The mountains bowed towards you and turned into a towering waterfall into which you fell, your roar of terror submerged by the elemental roar of the waters. But the waters calmed and assumed a great silence as they rose into the skies, only to re-form into an erupting volcano. Reptiles climbed its scaly surface, turning to grin at me. Only this grin distinguished them from the red carapace of the volcano itself.

I looked for you inside the gasping red pustule of the volcano and saw you falling, falling, a mere flint within the churning elements. The black ash that hailed down from the red mouth formed into characters which faded before I could understand their meaning.

I did not know whether these fearsome visions were dreams or a kind of super-reality. I knew later that I had fallen ill, that I lay in bed and was forbidden to see you. I seemed to travel through many seas and many skies in a week of sickness. Whenever my mind surfaced, one thought remained.

The question you had asked my father had instantly betrayed you.

From my bed I heard the whispering in the streets, as people began to read all sorts of things into my illness. The more superstitious among them said I had lost my reason, that the family had begun the celebration of arcane, mystical rites, and that the downfall of the government was imminent, of which my decline was a signal.

It was a signal to me, it was true. A signal to get well and get back to my work on the streets. When I left the house I sensed - with an invalid's delicate perception – that the air had become clearer, less opaque, that the numbers of people crammed into boxes, like human parcels in a living cemetery, had grown. That their faces were more eloquent.

I did not linger there, however. I had to prove to everyone that I was well.

My friends in the Glass Houses didn't refer to my reported state of insanity. Instead they asked about my travels to Europe, England and America, as they always did. It was our habit, after taking a trip abroad, to share experiences, but now their descriptions seemed to be so superficial. I grew silent after an hour or so of hearing about elegant casinos and beaches resembling white silk.

They were always somewhere else, in places that became unreal through long telling. My life with these people, whom I had known since childhood, was now remote. I saw that growing up had nothing do with it. These people, these friends, would remain children even when they were shot dead in the streets by the communists.

I continued to humour them as magnificently plumed birds wandered among us, pecking the bread from our hands, making me feel as though my mood itself had taken bird form, while street vendors brought cosmetics and jewellery on gilded trays with the obsequious bow of harem eunuchs.

And then you appeared.

In your arms was a dead child.

The ladies screamed and stood up, pushing back their little gilded chairs.

"Not here!" one of them screamed. "This is an exclusive area. How dare you bring beggar corpses into this neighbourhood!"

You ignored the storm gathering around you, and your eyes were fixed clearly on me. They burned with a strange radiance. I could not stop the thought: what has this to do with me? It was as though you had brought the dead boy in answer to the questions I had posed to myself about the false glamour of the life I had lived up till now.

"Where are his parents?" I asked. You shrugged. "An orphan, I guess. Who knows. just a child of the streets. A hit-and-run driver in a Porsche knocked him down."

We carried the boy home. As I looked down on him I could see the little girl whose face I had touched in the street just before I became ill.

We dug a grave for him beneath eucalyptus trees and high white stones which threw black shadows across the pathways in the heat of August.

CHAPTER TEN

The Spell

My thoughts turned to that day in the factory square. After the cigarette girl had finished dancing I went off alone to check the car - you had to be careful in such places. The break was over. You could hear the girls laughing as they returned to work. The street noises dwindled to an occasional shriek or giggle. The crickets were louder in my ears now. And louder still, the silence of the mountains bearing down on me.

But not loud enough to drown the thud of the rose she had thrown at you.

It left a mark on your face. I could see it clearly when you came up to the car where I was waiting for you. It was like a stigmata. The ecstasy of freedom I had experienced on that day alone with you evaporated. I felt a vague bleakness.

That was me. How stupid I had been, waiting for the right moment. Waiting for you to lose the habit of drink. Doing nothing.

There was a fine layer of red dust on the car. The notice I had placed on the inside back window had come unstuck and was flapping away in the hot breeze. The notice told drivers in bold black ink to avoid hitting the street children.

I must fix it with sellotape, I thought.

I had forgotten my sunglasses. I shielded my eyes with my hand, but the red rose was there behind the black space of my hand. It made a perfect "O" like a lipsticked mouth glistening. "What kept you?" I asked. You were looking down at your feet, avoiding my eyes. Then you opened the car door and started to brush yourself. Brushing something away. Her red lips. The O of the rose.

As though she had kissed you.

"She kissed you," I said.

"Fucking gypsy," you muttered.

You sat there in your fine pale grey suit. Not sweating, despite the heat. The immaculate cuff of your white shirt gleamed as the sun hit it, throwing out light sparklets from the gold cuff-links. Leaving me to interpret the silence.

Your delicate hand - not rough from the fields, but placid and long-fingered - drummed gently on the car window. It irritated me. I opened the convertible roof and drove fast to feel the hot breeze ruffling my hair.

The notice at the back of the car flapped and flapped like a trapped chicken and finally flew away.

Now we were staring down at the child's grave and I realised we were still holding hands. Suddenly the Carmen incident seemed insignificant. We had come some way together, after all. I was ashamed of feeling jealous in the face of the boy's death. I was ashamed that he reminded me of the little girl I had touched in the street. As though even in death his identity had been scrubbed out.

Yet the little girl's face disturbed me more than the boy's death. And then I knew who she reminded me of: Carmen. The same wild eyes staring into her own soul. Those lips pushing out her face so that they seemed to be both laughing and crying at the same time.

A desperate inside-out face.

I had seen her as beautiful. Her and the child. I now saw how ugly they both were with the ringworm of their poverty twisting inside them. They seemed briefly one and the same.

My grandmother had told me about twin souls. I used to sit in school trying to make my soul drift away at will, wondering how many times you'd have to come back to this earth to find your twin soul.

Were these two twin souls - innocent child and manipulative woman at the same time?

You grasped my shoulders and turned me towards you. Your eyes seemed opaque, like blind peoples' eyes so that you don't know what part of their face to look at.

You said you thought we should get married. To please your mother. You had been brought up to observe a strict code of ethics. I had saved your life and those of your parents. The one who saves your life owns it.

You said, however, there were difficulties. You understood that status got in the way. It would be impossible. But then you added: "Now do you understand about my drinking?"

I nodded slowly. With my free hand I caressed your hair, the black forelock that kept spilling into your eye. I ran my hand down your taut back which always made me think of a child bracing himself for a reprimand. You were locked into yourself, with an Asiatic completeness that evoked a great tenderness within me.

We lay down beside the child's grave. And it was here that we made love for the first time. The hard, dry earth pressed into my body as I lay beneath you. It gave the sex between us an intense lustre. It was a sex that revealed us more to ourselves than to each other. Your sighs and muffled words came from some other place within you, a place intimated at but not attainable.

And you said the words I have never been able to forget - that you would think of me on the point of your death.

I knew, then, that I was making love to a man already under the spell of another woman.

That night 3000 guerrillas led an insurrection against the army. Machetes in hands, they moved with one intent towards the town. All night long the air, overlaid with a fine shroud of volcanic ash, sighed with the screams of the victims. Small farting sounds of gunfire, too rude, too impudent to cause such carnage. I heard feet running, voices yelling.

We lay under the bed inside the white palace that was the seat of all our power, holding hands, trembling. I kept thinking of the story of the princess and the pea. The real princess would feel the pea beneath the weight of all the bedclothes. Could such refinement help me to feel the true edge of the earth that you felt - that coarse surface on which all empires must one day crumble?

You wanted to go to find your family in the village. I persuaded you to wait.

"What use is a dead man to them?" I asked.

My father and brother met with other members of the ruling classes. The army came into our house. I heard the goose-stepping of their boots, the clash of steel and drums in their voices. They frightened me more than the noise of the guerrillas outside. My father argued frequently with Alvarez over a tactical response. My brother, apt to become hysterical like our mother, took a hard-line approach and had to be calmed by my father, whose experience in these matters – or so he said – inclined him towards a wait-and-see approach.

For the past week I'd had a recurring dream of an army band mustering its hardware and inexorably moving towards me, flags and hands and feet keeping time, slicing the air with flashes of steel and nearer still, the rat-tat-tat of the band until I knew it was me they were coming for with musket, fife and drum and the unstoppable weight of military power, ready to trample me, to crush me underfoot.

But in the house the soldiers sat down quite sedately, sipping local brandy as though nothing was happening in the world outside our villa. Now and again the conversation was stirred by someone with a bit more passion into the intensity of debate.

Then I remembered the look in my father's eye during the single conversation he'd had with you.

"A minor insurrection," he said. "A little pogrom, that's all. We can contain it."

In the days that followed, the spatter of gunfire and snipers' bullets continued.

The servants risked their lives in the streets to buy provisions. Nobody thought anything of it. Bread was baked and filled the house with the reassuring smell of life being firmly kneaded together.

The diurnal rhythms of housework resumed. The brass was polished even more vigorously than usual. And the marble floors were washed down several times a day, even on the days when there were no military conferences.

My mother kept an eye on the housekeeper who kept an eye on the servants to make sure that all the work was done properly. As though she had caught the rhythm of the house my sister played the piano without a pause and her eyes reflected an old, deep awareness I had not seen in her for years. She played mostly Bach. And sometimes Bizet. When she started playing the song that Carmen had sung to seduce the crowd, your back grew rigid and you drummed your fingers on the windowsill.

At dawn the serving girls were on their knees with

buckets of water swishing the shiny marble as they began washing the floors. A regiment of skinny behinds moving along the hallway. It was, in effect, a military operation. Not one was out of sync with another. They were not allowed to hold the hand-rail on the staircase for support as they walked up and down with their burdens of brushes and polish and air sprays, lest their bitter hands stain the brass with the evidence of their toil.

My mother stood there, hands on hips, emulating the army major in a high staccato voice, despite her flowing nightgown and high-heeled slippers. Her nit-picking ways had begun to eat into her beauty. Deep lines of discontent had begun to spread in two estuaries down the sides of her face.

Our house had many corridors. Voices echoed everywhere. Everything could be heard. Words were never intimate. They existed to shatter the silence, rather than warm the house. Everywhere you could hear the sound of feet on stone. An endless shuffle to nowhere. From childhood this house had made me aware of the restlessness of human life and the cold eternity of stone - broken sometimes by the sound of my mother crying. Her emotions did not touch me. Why, I thought, is she crying when she has everything? Even though the house itself had told me she had not.

Yet I remembered how my grandfather's death had affected her - and the way she was suddenly filled with a burden of bedtime stories that she disgorged to us each night. The hobgoblins and evil fairies, princes and noble spirits trapped into the bodies of voracious beasts clearly gave her more nightmares than they did her children who were the recipients of these tales.

Once I found her on her knees by her bed, praying that she would not outlive me. My grandmother was standing at the doorway.

"What will be will be," she said.

CHAPTER ELEVEN

The Lovers

Now that we were lovers, we thought of little else. We would find bizarre places to love in, if not cemeteries and military courtyards, then the glass menagerie of the deserted square. Once we climbed the belfry of the church tower. Then we returned, holding hands, to your bed or mine in the creaking darkness behind locked doors, evading the patrolling staff.

I would bury my face in your hair, smelling it, hoping to become the smell of it, root of its root. I wanted you physically and invisibly; I wanted to you to be intangible, like a ghost, and plausible, like my own voice.

And sometimes, I wanted distance. In those times I made you pose for me for hours, as I painted you, but I could not get your likeness. I saw the formation of your lips, like a natural escarpment in the rock, rigid as the Sphinx but with a hint of a smile. Rushing towards me yet retreating at the same time.

How deep is it? How far out is it? My art professor used to question, holding a plumb line from the model's nose to measure height, space and density, until he resembled a priest swaying an incense burner between a line of worshippers.

The civil war continued. Yet I felt no warning stirring

within you. It was as though, having gained your body, and something of your fractured, dispirited ego on canvas, I became a stranger to your spirit.

"It's time you left." My father said.

You stood up, facing him in a swiftly fading military posture. It was as though you had only just arrived in our house, had never even sat down in it. You were the stranger who does not expect a welcome. You nodded briefly and thanked him for his hospitality. Your tall, slender body of a young oak tree seemed so breakable. Your face already had a distant expression and I knew that what so drew me towards you was the very imminence of your loss.

But I was the one to break the silence.

"I'm coming with you."

"Don't be silly. There is no point."

How often have I mulled over such words. Why did you say there was no point? Why didn't I insist that there was a point?

Measure the distance, said the art master. Examine the depth.

You demeaned me, made me feel that I was not up to sharing the burden of the responsibility you had taken upon yourself. The words returned, swooping like a bird of prey. What can it mean to say there is no point? It is a kind of abandon, expressing one's apartness from the other person. Such words set up their own dreadful resonance in the universe. There is no point. A tiredness, a giving in, a throwing up of hands.

Nevertheless you wrote to me after you left us. But you gave no forwarding address. You told me gung-ho stories I only vaguely believed. How you had narrowly escaped being imprisoned for desertion. Once you passed an army jeep carrying Carmen. She had been convicted of causing grievous bodily harm, having knifed a work-mate in a fit of temper. She eyed you mulishly. Her hands were tied behind her back. She wore a red skirt. Her white blouse was torn and dishevelled with blood on it.

Only later you remembered where you had seen her before.

Here is another scenario. I spent a night pleading with my father. I told him there could be no other man in my life but you. After that he finally gave in, and agreed that that we should both leave for Europe.

My father knew that years of politics, business and the maintenance of power had greyed his spirit and made him distant from simple things. Somehow our passion had touched his soul.

But in Paris you became unnerved by rudeness and hostility, and swore viciously at the cleaners who knocked on the door despite the "Do Not Disturb" notice and the waiters who came by with such clatter to take our trays away.

You started rows in restaurants because you couldn't stand the mincing steps of the waiters or the raw, pink duck in the shallows of a white porcelain platter, sprigged with watercress, or the feeling that an almond-eyed man at the next table, who had been watching your behaviour with amused interest, fancied you.

So we hired a car and drove east across Europe where sunflower fields linked the two halves of the continent like a sliced lemon. Crumbling masonry, stony baroque beauty, this was the sad legacy of Europe's war in the east, you said. You drank less. Sober, you stared at the grey walls pock-marked with bullets and heard the ghost of war-songs, the sigh of air-raids, the calm that was like an intake of breath. You said you could feel the interior disintegration of such cities in your own life.

"Only because you look for it," I said.

Like Sheherezade I told surreal stories to calm your sadness and to hold you to me. They were always about us. We would be found in the spires of Prague cathedrals, or floating, locked together along the course of the Danube, and only people who understood this passion could actually see us in flight, and they said it was the astral projection of two great lovers whose real selves are elsewhere, performing boring, mundane tasks, perhaps eating their lunch, perhaps dead. Yet even astral projections did nothing to lighten your inner darkness. I felt it in the plane going home, sitting beside you in the first class section, watching the stewardess in her little dumb-show with oxygen mask and life-jacket, just so, with the hands, pulling the mask down over the nose, and another little mime with the life-jacket, the hands indicating fore and aft, port and stern, her smile, abstracted, her make-up smooth, glibly rehearsing the crash which would propel us all with our dinner on our tray straight into God's lap.

How often have I travelled this way, the bodyguards behind me, fear in the pit of the stomach, lifting and merging with the swell of the plane. Soon little icicles will gather on the window through which I see the friendly earth with its grass and its seas tilt and arch away until it becomes a compact disc.

But, turning to see the spin of the earth in your eyes, you were, of course, not with me.

As you were not in the Louvre, nor the Czech cathedrals reaching stubbornly for the stars.

I was travelling alone, consigned to Europe like a 19th century European heiress, in the naive belief that travel mends a broken heart and returns a muffled mind to its senses.

❧

There had been no bending towards the light by my father. No softening of his heart. You went away because he sent you. I was alone. My mother called it infatuation, a mere crush. I would get over you in time.

"I never want to hear his name spoken in this house", said my father.

"If he ever sets foot in this house again, I'll kill him", said my brother.

I returned from Europe. I met my friends who were drinking iced tea and giggling among the peacocks who came by, strutting and posing. My friends asked incessant questions about the fashions in Rome and Paris. They named famous names, asking me which celebrities I had met. Their incessant questions exhausted me.

Don't speak of our love, you told me, or you sell it. Those words, which had seemed so soulful at first, now sickened me. They were the cynical remarks of a fleeing lover.

I watched the street children. They watched me. I felt unable to do anything for them. I feared they would grow up with their small trust broken.

How can it end so abruptly? I felt like a piece of lost property, discarded and then returned to its original owners. I stared at the familiar people, diminished in your presence, but who now filled my life again with all their old, forgotten complaints and petty anxieties.

He was not for you, said my mother, a gravedigger spading earth over the dead. Not your class, dear.

We knew it would happen, your father and I. We said nothing. But we knew.

He drank, didn't he? said my father, mildly inquisitorial.

The drink. Pulled by the gravity of drink. Weigh it against your impossible wealth, you once quipped. Can't you stop? It drags me down, I replied.

And you are a ball-breaker you retorted.

And despite the pain I wanted to paint. But I couldn't.

CHAPTER TWELVE

Partings

You had left everything neatly hung and folded in your wardrobe. The silk shirts that fell like a whisper from your hand, painted with hieroglyphics, the neckties of luminous colours, the finely-cut suits you never wore.

They should have made me believe in your return. Instead they were like the clothes of a dead man that you flinch from touching because they so confirm the fact that he's never coming back.

"And another thing," said my father. "You can stop this sentimental nonsense of feeding the poor in the streets. You make yourself ridiculous, lowering yourself - you, an aristocrat - squatting in the streets with the scum."

When I was with you I had colluded with you against them, hating their narrow views, their fear of the poor, even when it felt uncomfortable, disloyal, to do so. Now you had left it was so easy to do the opposite, to change perspective and console myself with seeing only your faults. Even to believe my father was right. And I began to wonder whether I had ever really seen you at all. Being close to someone is merging with them. Not really seeing them.

I doubted whether I would ever be with you again.

Sometimes I could still smell the whisky that had made you lucid for a while like a candle until it flickers out. If only you could have remained in this lucid state, without it being drink-induced, I thought, but I knew that states of mind are fluid, always moving towards something else, bigger or smaller.

I told you that I used to dream of parallel lines, roads that never converged, that I could not make the choice of which line to take. You replied that was us, you and me, parallel lines, love and respect, seduction and holding back, Venus, whore, but more of Venus, and it was Venus which made it impossible for the roads ever to meet, not the whore.

All these things came to me when I wasn't thinking of anything, when I was just moving, a moving object, for that was all I had become.

You also said I had a tendency to exaggerate the good things and that the two roads had another meaning - that I had to face reality which was hard for me because of my status. I hated those harsh, divisive words of yours.

But then you said we shouldn't waste what little time we had because when it was over it was really over, and nothing is as dead as dead love, it has more death in it than the side of pork hanging, fly-ridden from the butcher's nail.

The point is that you continued to write, even though with no forwarding address. You wrote as a fugitive still, and at the mercy of people you could never quite trust. You had grown a moustache, looked older. You had one or two grey hairs. You described gringos you had met who spoke of a better life. Guerrillas who talked airily of having blown bridges and taken villages.

But gradually the excitement of reading these letters to which I could not reply began to isolate me. They had nothing to do with us any more.

In the empty courtyard the sun rose and threw a black shadow upon me. My grandmother was looking at me in a way that made me catch my breath. I saw myself in her. I saw the eyes that grew brighter, the eyelids heavier with unused-up love, the body contracting, the hands becoming papery, so there and yet not there - all of her reduced by this great burden of love.

And I saw my mother who had folded away her beauty on the first day of the menopause as a bride folds away her wedding dress.

I wanted to run to both of them, to throw myself into their arms and beg them not to let anything like this happen to me.

"What does he write - what does he write?" persisted my grandmother. I saw the pleasure she derived from looking at me begin to pale into this shared pain. For in the innocence that returns with age she understood, in the way my mother could not. I looked back at her and became as she was then, light and transparent as a leaf.

"I was his lover," I replied. "But now there is nothing to say. His letters are his future and my past."

She took my hand and whispered: "Don't become like your mother."

I understood the fist of anger in my mother's heart for the man who had estranged her. Suddenly I felt a wave of inexpressible love for her.

It grew dark. I walked into the night and felt the desert breathe. I read each breath. Each one said, yes I am here. I am always here. I have been here for ever.

A fox darted between the silent volcanoes - a child playing hide and seek between indulgent parents.

And this at least made me smile.

CHAPTER THIRTEEN

Letters Home

It appears that we made love once. Many times, yes, but in truth only once. Of course I did not understand this until Carmen entered your life. After that your letters changed. And I was sad when I remembered our love among the tombstones.

I can't explain how this girl began to penetrate your letters. She had escaped jail and was now the leader of some form of protest movement. There was danger around her. A wild secrecy. Grenades, minefields, leapt from the pages of your letters. And always this sense of going out into the dark on unspecified missions. What were you doing, José? What was your role in all this?

If you were really mixed up in something so dangerous, I wondered how you dared write. How your letters had not been intercepted. And yet it was all so vague. I read and re-read the words carefully and could come to no firm conclusion. Was it fantasy or madness, I wondered. The product of drugs or drink?

You avoided the use of her name. But she was there on every page. A girl. A woman, whose shape, whose very essence, grew with each letter you wrote.

It made me feel like a small child staying up late to peep at the adults downstairs at play. Watching them ends your childhood. Now the waiting days collapsed. The daylight wouldn't fade; the dark night refused to lighten. Everything I looked at was in its absolute, unchanging state, as though nothing would ever begin or end again.

One day soon, I felt, I shall shake off this paralysis which holds me here, recumbent, reading your letters with a bitter-sweet fatalism. Some day a small flame will ignite inside me and I will know who I am. I will raise myself out of my lethargy and walk out of the house that binds me to my old life, listening to the old arguments of home, to my sister's rapturous music and inner silence, to my grandmother's Delphic somnambulance, to the tedium of long out-grown friendships.

I visited an analyst. She sat, wall-eyed, voice down, knees interlocked like two snakes. A perched notebook on those sharp knees. Her flat gave off a false air of sparseness, for it was actually filled with everything - books, Asian artefacts, American furniture. A clock ticked. I was placed several feet away from her, so that she had to squint and bend her head forward to hear me.

She took up the open ends of my sentences, and reversed them in my direction, using the first or third person to address me.

"And so José left me?" she enquired. " So how did that make me feel?"

She continued in her soft, hypnotic voice as I sat holding my face in my hands.

"What are my true feelings about myself? About me - Michaela?"

The analyst had a trio of alabaster elephants on an onyx table and a box of tissues because her clients sometimes cried.

"You can't help me", I burst out. "You can't give me back the smell of his hair, the quality of his sigh when he said I knew how to please him, his irritable, drunken moan of self-loathing from the next room, even the rumble of his stomach, and the way he would lurch, half-dressed, towards the door, and put a finger on his mouth when he heard someone outside."

"What does Michaela really want?"

"I want him back. Isn't that obvious?"

"When the earth moves," she said, "it can't slip back into its old place again."

I stopped visiting the analyst. I saw her later in the street but she no longer remembered me. She passed me like a stranger. I stared back at her. I thought of her as a suitcase walking away with me inside her. And you - how you would laugh, though, if you knew.

"Look at it this way," you said when I was still a virgin. You put two matchboxes together and buttressed them with a third.

"These two are the lovers. The third box is the sex. The lovers are cemented together by the sex. Sometimes the sex represents a third party. Don't look so shocked. That third party, that secret, adulterous affair or love of three lovers, binds the experience even tighter. Do you see? Do you understand? Don't give me that blank look. You are not as young and innocent as you pretend to be. No-one is who has seen what you have seen."

Abruptly you changed mood and put the matchboxes back in your pocket. Your face looked glum. From another pocket you pulled a pack of cards and shuffled them to form a fan. Then you put them away, too, with the smooth dazzle of a conjurer.

The black shadow descends within the courtyard at midday as the *cicadas* click out their endless rat-tat-tat. The shadow is the lonely shadow of my grandmother. And I leave the house, just to get away. I pass the everyday places. The small station behind the hot, damp cluster of trees. Behind them comes the sound of a woodcutter whose work is punctuated by the rhythmic da-di-da-di-da of a passing train, louder and louder, drowning out every noise until it, too, dies away and the unchanging thump of the woodcutter is heard once again. Beyond that I begin to hear the faint rustle of the traffic and the street life.

These are my sounds. These are the sighs and breaths which I would weld into a symphony if I were a composer.

It was you who opened my eyes to my innocent extravagance and to the poverty of my countrymen. Once I had pushed aside insistent children in rags with old, hard faces, failing even to notice their inventiveness. I barely noticed how they juggled, they raced, they clowned, they told jokes. How they straddled the traffic lights and stood on each other's shoulders, silently grinning at the crowds with a mouth full of bad teeth and the performer's terse dignity. Where? In places where I didn't see them. Under the Christmas lights of trees hung with the candy-filled Bufana doll for the rich kids to beat down with sticks so that they could fight over the spoils of confectionery. Our streets lay open and corruptible. Policemen sauntered by with evil leers; girl soldiers guarded the Treasury building, swishing their pony tails and adjusting their machine-guns slung over their backs, and beyond the consular avenues whose mansions were built from black volcanic ash, you could feel the sickness of the countryside, deep and treacherous.

America was the dream, the ice-cream dream whose border was light years away. Old women still crossed themselves yet there seemed no Christ, no God in this land, yes a God-ridden land, you said when I described for you the church-going Sundays of my childhood, parading the streets in all our finery, the villagers gaping at us, my father belting out the hymns in a sanctimonious baritone, but that was before the priests became insurgents and fled for their lives, leaving the churches to tower in silent rectitude over the sacks of corn and other provisions which had been piled up inside their vestries with the triumphalism of matter over spirit.

When I have grown up, I asked, what will I see? Only poverty? Only the need to redistribute wealth? And what then? When you have redistributed all the wealth, will it really make anyone less hungry? Or will it just make another set of people hungry instead? And you with your drink, I went on, you are hardly the puritan reformer!

I drink to forget, you said.

Me. To forget me?

Carmen took over. There she was, alive on the page. The notepaper on which you had scrawled your letter, as though in a hurry to be through with it, stank of her perfume. I sat in my room calling her names to burn out my anger and also because if you name something, you have it by the scruff of the neck, you break its power. Not so hers.

I saw the fox again when I walked out to the mountains, later at moonlight. A pair of gleaming eyes which, for one moment, seemed to see me. I had the odd feeling that it was you. Maybe both of you together. A fleeting transmigration of souls.

I want to tell you about the fox. I want to laugh again and become me again with you. I want to tell you how it felt to walk, after you had been inside me, aching all over, and filled with your being, your being inside me. And it was funny, this ache, it made me laugh and cry at the same time because it felt as though I was carrying you around all the time, more than a memory, a presence, and that can never go, although of course it does because there will be others, I want to tell you, for both of us.

I don't feel it now, but of course there will be others. Will there be?

I had never told you that before. About these sensations of the body. It felt rude. I was too refined, you said. Too refined to show emotion. It came out in other ways, crying all the time. Crying over the dead boy. Crying about what you had shown me in the streets, the streets I had always known, with the beautiful gardens backing onto them like a tantalising future these people will never see. Unless and unless. Here we go again. You are always so political. Can't you ever *not* be serious? You have known me all your life, you said stiffly. Like you have known these back streets. And you never took any notice until I opened your eyes.

I wanted anger. I wanted anger enough to kill.

I became troubled by thoughts of the analyst I visited. I remembered thinking of her as a suitcase walking away with my life - so the you that is in me is also in that suitcase. Walking away.

CHAPTER FOURTEEN

The Power

In your next letter you were more specific. You wrote that you had joined the Movement. You had been summoned to an interview. That letter was particularly nervous. A sense of drumming fingers on a desk etched with peoples' initials. The graffiti took you back to your schooldays - sponsored by the wealthy ladies of the city who had formed a charitable trust to provide education for poor children. You hated school, wanting only to be in the fields helping your mother. Sometimes you were forced to stand behind your desk, with your hands behind your head for some trivial misdemeanour. You used to read the letters scratched into the desk surface and devise names and personalities for them.

Now you glanced down to the desk where you were waiting to be interviewed, and saw that someone had, with more than usual artistry, etched the initials, C and J, into the old wood. And you were filled with foreboding. At that moment Carmen entered the room. She had a red beret slung over her glossy black hair.

Suddenly she tripped at the door, cursing and glaring at everyone had witnessed the incident. You saw in her face a twist of destinations, a confluence of rivers.

She sat down, looked up. Peremptory at first, but then

came a softening of her face. A mumbled apology for her outburst hovered in the air. Questions she asked that you can't remember now. She folded back her hair behind one ear as she bent over the notepad to write down your answers. Her face in shadow suddenly seemed deep and intense.

Contrary to my opinion, she was not beautiful, you said. You thought I might like to know. As though the word 'beautiful' contained both the mystery and the mastery of love.

Sitting opposite her at the desk you began to sense a feminine force more powerful than you had ever known.

You said that the political turbulence now rocking our land was female. The will to destroy had distorted the will to nurture but the destruction was necessary because it made way for a rebirth. Feminism and other political catalysts were only symptoms, not the cause of this sudden thrust of female energy.

I could see Carmen, with her red beret at an acute angle. And then I saw her at home. A room with a violent protest poster and a red rose. Black cushions scattered untidily. Weapons of war. I paint you this picture in my imagination.

What a cliché - I hear you taunt. How little you understand!

I walk slowly through the courtyard, clutching your

letter. I feel numb. The gardener, who always annoys me with his sly looks, mutters something inaudible. A servant is sleeping under a broad sombrero. The splayed feet proclaim this puny independence - this right to take a siesta in the heat of the day. There is a shadow thrown by the bougainvillaea against the wall under the thick afternoon sunlight. The *cicadas* click away. Life seems in suspension.

I enter the house, blinking in the extreme darkness caused by the contrast of the light outside. The sounds vanish. Peace. I walk quietly to my room, hoping not to be accosted on the way. It is so quiet now that from my grandmother's room I can hear her turning the pages of a magazine. I close the door to my room and tears well up. I think of the places of our lovemaking. The masked words. We were less honest than our bodies. We knew. The body rarely dissembles, and knows what is meant for eternity and what is temporal. Then why am I crying?

You cry for yourself, my grandmother would say. Not for him. If you love him, then love his freedom. But the hardest thing is to bring down to earth what has been so high in the sky, yet so fixed a point in your constellation. To guide it gently down and find a new focus for it.

But why your letters, José? What do you really want to tell me? Why can't you let go? Perhaps it is only because of your concern for your mother. In every letter you mention her, asking me to make sure she and your father are alright until you get back. It is a part of your letter I barely notice, yet when I do it seems to offer the most tangible hope. There is no address and no point of contact. Just this promise of a homecoming.

As for me, I can barely wait for the letters to arrive. I tear them open impatiently. Is it hope or masochism?

I knew I was changing. Looking back on my carefree life before you entered it I saw that what had burned most brightly in my firmament was in fact a black hole, swallowing everything. The light now came from something else - from a deep source within myself - this ability to feel and endure in silence.

I became aware of less perceptible things. Things bursting with their own momentum. The seasons changing. The dry twigs of winter throbbing with a silent vitality, understanding that nothing is really still in the air.

No death, you said. But the death was in us.

It was indeed as though our sexual love had died painlessly and without transition. You had built a wall between us. A wall of letters.

I thought of her. I imagined her. Taking my place and leaving me a shadow. I could smell her room. It had a laconic, coarse perfume. It was filled with her presence. Carmen.

I sat in my room thinking of the life being lived outside it. That day there were dried flowers in the vase. Beside it stood an alabaster carving of a horse that I had bought at an art auction. I had signalled my intention to buy with one finger of my gloved hand. I averted my face under a huge straw hat, and if that wasn't enough

I also wore a pair of dark glasses. People were curious. They always were. This time it was less for secrecy than a joke. You had been with me then. It felt so young - so vigorous, to take part in this little charade. You called me the Princess of Shades.

Of course I visited your mother. I put on a simple peasant dress and a scarf and I called on her. How much she had changed since my first meeting with her in the fields. Her eyes were hooded and both she and her husband moved slowly, furtively, as though in a dream from which they feared to awake.

She asked about you. She cried a little. I felt the child José growing up in their simple house. There was evidence on the walls of the work you had done at school, as though it were still necessary to prove that you had been educated. I saw the few home-made toys in your room, things made out of wood and raffia, painted in colours of fading brilliance.

We both asked so many questions of each other. They had lived in fear, following the killing of the foreman. Questioners, interrogators had come to the house with uniforms and raised voices. But they had not discovered a body.

It had all happened in one fortnight. That intense fortnight had changed them. They were relieved you had escaped, yet bitter at being left to face the consequences alone. Your desertion could have had them shot.

Your mother, I noticed, had a squint, so that I could never be sure when she was looking at me. It made talking to her difficult. Your going missing had cast a spell over the village. Strange dogs would appear in the night howling. Crops wouldn't grow. A malaise had settled like dust over the whole village.

In a sense they had buried you. They had made a mausoleum of your bedroom. I saw that it hardly mattered now whether you actually inhabited the earth; for them you were dead. Even though under my family's protection you had lived so near.

Only with me was your mother able to wring her hands and give full vent to grief and resentment. She sat in that poor house with its logs and simple, hand-made furniture and sobbed.

"Do you understand why I am angry at what he has done to us?" she asked.

"He prevented that foreman from killing you," I pointed out.

"It might have been better if he had," she said bitterly. I made no reply. She begged me to speak of you, to recreate you physically in her mind. Her features softened, radiating something of you and she rocked herself, hands tightly clasped around her, her white hair drawn back like fine wool around her head.

And we spent days like this. I would talk shyly at first, careful to avoid the word love. But gradually I realised that hearing her son described as lover gave her the full sense of his adulthood that had been so abruptly attenuated. So between us, mother and lover, the spectre of the missing son was nourished. Having dealt with your past, we did not speak of politics, but conjured up a mythical present tense based on your commitment to truth and justice. Neither of us mentioned drink, and I refused to discuss that name - Carmen. Even though I was dying to know more, wondered if she knew more than I did. It became clear to me that our positions had been reversed; your mother saw the man in you; I saw the child.

As we sat weaving lies and conjectures, your father pottered around, pulling his belt to hold up his dingy, scrappy trousers, shuffling, shifting, changing shape and filling the room with musty shadows as the day wore on and my mouth ached from talking. He was withdrawn from you - even from your mother - perhaps from some inner wisdom or prescience.

For your father took no part in our conversations. It was always his back, hovering as we spoke, not noticing how our hands darted like flames, our eyes filled with the heat of flames. Later I visited your cell-like room. I watched your childhood and adolescence unfold. Here were the parts I could not reach. Still, even now, I wanted to know you in a way no woman knows a man, nor mother, sister, neither. I tried stepping back and seeing you as an empty shell into which I had invested all kinds of wonderful things which actually had nothing to do with you. And then I considered whether I was simply in love with a self-created image. If so, it was too late - far too late.

I took a last, lingering glance at this room and felt a shudder of fear as I left. I kissed your mother and said goodbye. The smell of enclosed, sorrowful places emanated from her - from your home. I felt desperate to leave. She always elicited a promise from me to return soon. And she gave me letters to send you, not realising I had no forwarding address.

Years later, when I went through all your personal belongings, I was amazed at the accuracy of your replies to letters from her you had never read because, of course, I could not send them.

You told me to keep your memory alive for her. You asked me to go on seeing her. It gave you intense pleasure and some degree of satisfaction. I felt, then, like your wife. I was proud that you felt able to entrust me to preserve something of the character of your home. I kept her letters to you in a neat bundle under my bed.

CHAPTER FIFTEEN

Escape

Your next letter came from prison. It bore the marks of censorship.

You could not give me details, but it seemed you had been caught in some guerrilla activity. Carmen, you said, had got away. The rest of the letter was entirely bland. What time you got up. What you had to eat. How you had lost count of days, lost touch with reality and had no idea what was going on in the world. How can you love an ignoramus? you asked. Look, I wrote you a poem. Here it is.

Paper love, you wrote.
Floating downstream.
Of paper I dream.
Soundlessly in the dark cell,
I, floating downstream.
I am a river. The others,
Driftwood in my dream.

Do you like it? you asked. Do you understand it?

I went up to my grandmother's room and closed the door. José is in trouble, I told her. He needs papers, a passport and documentation. We need to prove that he is a member of one of the Families. She stared at me as though she had only just recognized who I was. Then she told me that there was a man named Sanchez who lived on the edge of the town who could help me.

"Your mother would say it is too dangerous," she added. "But I understand your need." And then after a pause: "But be careful not to love too well."

"You can trust Sanchez," she added, as an after-thought.

The man was sitting outside his house, his eyes screwed up against the harsh midday sunlight. He wore a pirate's kerchief on his head, which reduced his forehead to a narrow point above his squinting eyes and protruding nose. I saw the filigree lines around his eyes and his narrow lips. He appeared a disreputable character and I began to wonder what had persuaded my grandmother to lead me to him, but then I found myself held in his gaze, which was clear and intelligent.

I told him I needed his help to get someone out of prison. The cost was not in question. He slowly fiddled with a worn leather purse.

"Political?" he asked with a grim smile.

"Isn't everything?"

He continued to study me for a moment, and then stood up awkwardly, arthritically, holding his side and entered his house. He closed the door. After some time he returned with a large, crumpled envelope which he began to seal with his tongue. When it wouldn't close he thumped it, cursing. He thought for a moment and then wrote something on it.

"This is for the Chief of Police," he said. "For his eyes alone."

I took it to the office of the Chief of Police in the main square. It was here that years ago the bodies of the *campesinos* were hung on meat hooks outside the butchers' shops and sold as pork. A sense of horror and outrage had clung to the air for months afterwards. A whole town refused to eat meat since the vision of their fallen countrymen would not die and nightmares became tangible daily events in the street.

Some said that the massacre of 30,000 insurgents had evoked memories of the mass sacrifice of our tribal ancestors, and for days the sound of shuffling feet could be heard, which people described as the sacrificial March of Days.

In the police chief's office I stared out of the window where the soldiers marched up and down, the same women soldiers with swinging pigtails I had last seen when you and I had taken that fateful drive out of town when we met Carmen. Their drill was somewhat laconic, pierced by an occasional giggle. Police chief Zuniga was scratching his signature on a letter and did not look up as I entered.

When he did, his eyes travelled all over my body. I wore a brilliant red suit with a tapering skirt and wide-brimmed hat. My face was expressionless. He stared at me for several moments. It was a glance filled with admiration, and desire bounded with respect.

It took him some moments to speak. The lewdness of his stare was intensified by the fact that he did not make eye contact with me. He touched his moustache absently with his pen.

"What can I do for you, Señorita ?" he asked, at last.

"After you have read this letter I need you to facilitate my next move," I said.

He fingered his moustache again and then opened the envelope. He glanced up even more evasively this time, as he took out the letter and smoothed it on the desk before reading it. Then he cleared his throat, drummed his fingers alongside the letter and sat back. He looked at me.

"Is this really necessary, Señorita?" he asked after a moment. "I mean, a prisoner ... "

"A prisoner of no importance," I declared abruptly. "Of no possible value to the State. One who represents no threat whatsoever."

"In your view, Señorita."

I stood up and pushed back the chair angrily.

"Do you doubt my political acumen, Señor?"

"Don't misunderstand me, Señorita. I know your family well. Of course I am fully aware..."

"Not sufficiently aware, Señor Zuniga," I snapped. "Had you been better informed this arrest would not have taken place and you would not now be questioning my reasons for intervening in a matter that could incur you considerable political embarrassment. The man you have arrested is a guest of my family. You have made a mistake, Señor."

He sighed, emitted a short laugh of surrender and threw up his hands.

"How would you like me to proceed, Señorita?"

"I think the terms for the man's release are explicit in the letter, Señor. If you expedite the matter, there will be no further comeback."

Zuniga gave a short sigh, opened the drawer under his desk and took out a letterhead on which he proceeded to write. He signed his name, folded the letter in an envelope, stood up and bowed smartly as he handed it to me.

"I think you know to whom to give this, Señorita?"

I took the letter, inclined my head slightly and he moved to the doorway to usher me out.

As I passed out of the door I felt his light touch on my arm.

"Forgive me, Señorita," he said, "But are you sure you are not making a mistake? You are a young and beautiful woman, a prominent member of society. This action will cause you deep regret in later years. I know this as I know the ways of the world."

"Speak of this to no-one and your position is safe," I told him.

I left his office light-headed. I had taken from him what I wanted. Nobody would ask questions.

I heard the cafes coming to life on the other side of the square; the girl soldiers paraded up and down with a touch of the flirt in their stride. I sat down at one of the cafes and watched. It seemed that only I could sense beyond this the cardboard city; the dark and hungry faces; the limbs rising slowly from their boxes of sleep. I felt them around me, the eyes wild and not those of a child but an old man, old men, cadaverous old men. I could see them from here, standing on each other's shoulders like circus clowns, throwing out their hands for money, putting coins greedily in their tattered pockets, but no smile of pleasure in their sad-clown faces or their small, squat bodies. I dreaded the traffic lights where they would gather soundlessly, waiting for me, always waiting. And behind them, like some hideous effluence, the mothers lying limp and exhausted, suckling their hopeless young, suckling them to become sellers of cocaine, too lethargic to jostle, too innocent to escape their fate. I had felt powerful in the police chief's office, but now they came past me, like lepers, like open sores, and I saw something that I had not seen even with you, José. I saw this hole, this cavern opening up in the midst of humanity and then the figure of Carmen walked into it and stood there, laughing with her hands on her hips, all sex, for it is only sex and always sex that transcends status and equalises and heals and nourishes and causes laughter to rise from the earth, laughter and pain, and then I knew that I and not her, for all her courage and all her politics, was the one closer to the disinherited, and a terrible, wasted feeling made me sink to my knees in the street and cry out. I saw then, as the poor people shuffled past all eyes, all eyes on me, and filling the street that had been full of cafes and good-looking soldiers, how vulnerable I was there, among these people, because a woman sinking to her knees in the street, be she princess or pauper, has no power and no status, but simply creates in herself another void in another space for people to peer down into, without pity and without interest, since they understand nothing.

As it happens, it was too late. The prison staff said you had gone. Days ago. Their interest had flagged. They had no concern for those sprung by interested parties, since it was beyond their scope. They only knew that corruption was like a serpent and could coil into the highest tree. To my incessant questions about your whereabouts they only shrugged, and went on smoking, eyeing the local women, passing lewd comments.

I waited until their tea break was over and only one man was left on duty. I opened my bag and calmly took out a wallet which I used as a fan as I approached him. "Perhaps you can tell me where I can find José?"

The information the man had given me led me through dark alleys and labyrinthine streets into an underworld I never knew existed. I could never have believed this strange city with grim, tumbledown buildings and menacing crowds lived parallel to my own. If I had wanted to turn back it would have been impossible for I would never have found the way. My path was waylaid with beggars. They stank and most were blind. Yet in their blindness I felt they saw me and knew me. Hands were stretched out to me at every turning, but I shrank from each one.

It grew dark. I began running. I did not know whether I was running towards or away from something.

I came to a house and stood outside it, breathless. As I looked at it, it appeared charming, like the Hansel and Gretel house, covered in sweets. Then I looked again and saw that they were not sweets but pungent flowers, covering the walls with bright colours.

Carmen was standing in the doorway, absently pulling at the flowers. There was a blast of flamenco music behind her. You were reclining on a sofa. Humming a song about flowers and twirling a dead rose. But I barely recognised you. You had changed, had grown heavier. You had taken shape from her.

"What the hell are you doing here, Michaela?" You burst out. You stared at her and then at me, smoothing down your hair, nervously.

"I heard you were here. I wanted to come. Actually I wanted to." I stopped and stared from one to the other.

I took out my purse, awkwardly, realising now that it was the wrong move. I looked at you with a small smile.

"I heard you were in prison. Thought you needed my help. All the way here I was scared. I kept going because somehow..."

I was unable to continue. Carmen's eyes bored through me, heavy and sardonic.

"But don't worry, José. I don't intend to try and buy you back."

"Buy him back?" asked Carmen.

Who the hell told you I was here anyway?" you countered.

"Don't be so naive, José. "

You glanced down at my purse and gave her a meaningful glance,

I hadn't meant it to seem this way. How clumsy it felt! Rattling purse strings to prove power. You and Carmen, you had all the power and I had none.

"Look, love," you said very carefully. "You must go. You know this is no place for you."

Love! You spoke the word with indifference.

"I should have come with you when you left our house, José. You stopped me. I shouldn't have listened. I had so many mixed feelings. So many confusions. All I know is I should be the one here with you."

I started to cry. You looked at her first, warily, then came to me slowly and put your arms around me. You had no feeling for me. Everything had gone. I stopped crying. I felt quite dry inside. You made me coffee, tried to pacify me. I felt I had been playing, all our times together. Again came that sense of being a child in the company of adults. How ice-cold this betrayal felt. You began muttering incoherently about some revolution you were planning, I couldn't grasp the full sense of it. It was like hearing something in a dream, a sort of overtone whose meaning remained elusive. I didn't know whether you were too embarrassed to make your meaning clear or whether you had been drinking again.

Carmen remained where she was, chewing on her flower and staring at me. I felt angry and bitter. But I also saw that she was not as daunting in her beauty as I had first thought.

She is too sloping in the body, her breasts are low, her stomach, too, sags a little, as though everything about her is being pulled to the centre of gravity. Yet she is at ease with herself. She has that bodily ease. That inner grace. I am awkward in my couture clothes; the red is too brilliant, too harsh. I look like a bony catwalk model, everything thrust out from the hip, everything contrived, derivative.

I can still see her in her little moccasins; not a particularly sexy image, it's true. That slightly Indian face, the slanted eyes and thin, muscular mouth, hardly lips at all until she pouts, and a long, curved, powerful nose that gives a sense of something almost vulpine.

"Generous of you to try and help us." The words unfurl from her mouth like smoke. "But you see, it wasn't necessary after all. We have excellent contacts, too, haven't we, José?" For a moment, as she looks down, I catch the sheer weight of her personality, the square, downward-turned face, the slightly varicose eyelids.

You spread your fingers in a dismissive gesture. She turns up the volume on the old cassette player that rattled out the flamenco music that drowned out your gentle song.

"Turn it off," you bellow at her.

"Don't order me around! I am boss around here."

And they begin to quarrel. Here they are, two political outcasts, two zealots, looking for a new world order. They raise their voices. José, you show a side I have never seen. You pull her towards you, menacing her. She swears at you. You throw her to the ground and raise a fist. She gasps, covers her face, then puts down her hand and looks you straight in the eye, unafraid.

"Stop it," I say. I pull you away from her. You try to push me off, then turn away from us both, ashamed to show your face.

"There was never this violence between us, José," I say.

"I know," you reply. "But this is different."

"Can't you remember how it was with us?" I plead. "Could anything have been more perfect? Why do you need to destroy such perfection, why must you taint it? You could spend a whole lifetime trying to capture the beauty of our relationship. And you throw it away!"

"What's over is over," says Carmen.

"Yes," you say. "I must throw it away."

You make a gesture of hopelessness.

I look at the passion between you, this sexual balance that I have upset simply by being there, and this gives me a small, inadequate sense of victory.

I look again and see that something nomadic emanates

from you both; something of the gypsy, the cocaine smuggler, something deeply out of touch with society, yet enriched with it, as a Bedouin may achieve wisdom from seeing the world pass through the yellow glaze of his desert.

But you have been nowhere. You have both grown up in a troubled land and found each other.

Carmen moves out of your grasp and smoothes down her long hair. She has a short, Indian body; she is slow, almost bovine, a whale moving through water, which will turn into a shark. She is also like a heavy jewel, rough from the quarry.

And suddenly she smiles. She seems encircled by an aureole of music. Her eyes darken suddenly and become black holes of such intensity that I cannot fight my way out. I struggle to avoid looking at her, but she is mesmerising. Gradually her story unfolds.

CHAPTER SIXTEEN

Carmen's Tale

Carmen had passed you in the jeep which was carrying her off to jail for having knifed another woman at work. You knew nothing of her political involvement at this time. Something, however, had drawn you to the place where the jeep was driving by. For some reason you stopped it and asked the driver for the name of a local village. He took out his map and his glasses and began searching for the name.

You and Carmen exchanged a glance which told you both that this was no chance meeting but the instrument of her escape. She remembers fixing you with her eyes before turning to the soldier who was guarding her and whispering something in his ear. She told him to look out for a eucalyptus tree on the way and bring a leaf of it home for her mother. It would cast a lucky spell on both the bearer and the recipient of the leaf. As the gullible soldier turned to look for the leaf, she leapt down from the truck so swiftly and silently that the soldier did not have the slightest inkling of what had happened.

While the driver pored over the map, quite unable to find the village which did not exist because you had made it up, the guard gave a yell and announced the prisoner's disappearance.

But she was already out of sight way beyond the trees before her absence was noticed and she had managed to weaken the string binding her hands by rubbing it repeatedly against the bark of the eucalyptus tree that did indeed bring her luck - although of course it did nothing for the guard, who subsequently spent six months in prison for allowing her to escape - well before the driver, swearing retribution, had decided which way to turn in order to find the prisoner.

You, José, were nearly knocked down by the furious jeep driver, he manoeuvred his vehicle into a near somersault in search of his quarry. Before any suspicion for the escape could fall upon you, you, too, ran in the direction of the trees, and there she stood, Carmen, like Eve with her apple, smiling seductively at you and thanking you for your hand in her destiny.

Their laughter as they recalled the event cleared the air between them but it also seemed tinged with nostalgia.

José's destiny belongs to both of us, she said, because he has been rescued by two women. My role however, she said, was over. Temporarily. Just for now.

What did that mean? I asked her.

"You will see, " she laughed. "But you must be patient."

Then she began fondling your hair. I looked away, amazed that I had even bothered to listen to her story, that I could remain there, mesmerised, too dull with pain to find the energy to leave, to say goodbye to you for ever, as I should have done.

There was much touching of hands between you. There was talk of missions. Other people came and went. They looked unshaven, uncouth. Carmen put thick carafes of red wine on the table. I saw coarse hands, blackened finger nails. People sat down talking for a few moments at a time. They drank, they leaned forward intently, they laughed raucously, showing layers of bad or missing teeth. Then they stood up to go. And others came, some bringing wine and tortillas. There was a great kinship among all the people who came to Carmen's table. I sat at the edge of it, like a novice, drinking in the atmosphere, watching all the people. I said nothing and no-one spoke to me. When I looked down I had the strange feeling that everything was happening in my life in the same place and the same time, that I could stay there and everything would pass through me and I could grow quietly old like that. It seemed an attractive proposition.

And then my feelings changed, and I became aware of my otherness, of a desperate vitality bouncing off onto me, and I felt the fierce rectitude of village women. And their immobility. I remembered my grandmother sitting by my bed telling me stories of the conquistadores, and of our own wild land shadowed by blood-red mountains whose ferocity was reborn in all the people of the Southern and Central Americas in every generation, and that this ferocity showed itself in even the gentlest people. Even in you, Michaela, she said. You will see one day.

Now I felt this ferocity. This ancestral presence. Suddenly I was my grandmother. I was her. Both ancient and young.

Carmen awakened me from this day-dream.

"Come", she said in her rough voice. She took me to another room. I hadn't tasted the wine, yet I felt drunk. She began to undress. She drew the blinds. In the pale light that darted between the slats, I saw her brown body. The legs were rather short, as I said before, but I had never seen such a softly moulded quality in any woman's body. As an artist, I wanted to paint her. She stood in silence for a moment, only her hands moving, unfolding a soldier's camouflage uniform. She put it on gracefully, her back firm and erect, in a movement that made me think of silk, rather than army camouflage. She shook out her long, black hair and piled it up into a cap. Then the face that looked at me was fierce and masculine, the lips pulled into a mean smile.

"Why did you call me into here?" I asked her.

"Do you understand the nature of our work, little one?" She took out a small knife from her belt and placed it under my chin.

"Do you have the stomach for it? Would you die for it?"

"You know who I am," I replied meaningfully, and wrenched the knife out of her hand.

"I came here to find José, not to die for your movement."

"Little oligarch! Little virgin!"

I threw the knife to the ground where it fell glittering and clattering. She laughed playfully. Her skin was dark

103

and evenly textured, with a luminescence which made you feel you were looking at a flame.

I wanted to see her not as a rival, not as a woman, even, but as someone on the path of adventure, in a state of motion. Yet she *was* a rival, and in the next moment I wondered why I had allowed her to usurp my own authority, to displace me without a fight.

I smiled at her nastily.

"No little virgin, Señorita."

Her mood changed abruptly. The sarcastic smile became bitter for a moment, but then, as though some elf of reason had whispered to her, she began to laugh. Then she pulled me towards her and took my hands with the rough warmth of a peasant, someone who sees no point at all in mystery. I watched her as though I were watching a film. Her lips were parted to reveal small, sharp animal teeth. I kept my eyes fixed on hers, trying to repel the magnetism that emanated from her. And then with a loud curse I freed myself and pushed her away.

"You are lucky," she said with a mischievous grin. "Usually Carmen eats her rivals."

And again her mood changed, and she stood up and smoothed down her uniform.

"Come, Michaela," she invited. "Let's sit here for a while and talk over a glass of wine."

She called out for one of the men to bring in a bottle with two glasses. Then as we sat together on the bed she studied me.

"You amuse me. I don't understand why José gave you up. You're a good-looking girl, especially when you fly into a rage. And as you say, you gave him a good life. He had everything he wanted with you. Too good, I would say."

"Aren't you jealous, then?", I enquired.

"Jealous? Me?" She laughed again, and poured us both a glass of wine. By now her speech was becoming a little slurred.

"Of all women I am not worth it. You see, they love so badly what they know is bad for them that they will pay dearly for it. They will renounce everything. Your José renounced the army. His home. Knowing he has put his family at risk. For what - for politics? For a vision of the future? Bah! That's all nonsense."

She leaned forward in a manner that was half confidential, half intimidating.

"I'll tell you something. My cause itself is nonsense. Every ideal, every possibility lives from one thing alone. Its sexuality. That is what I give him. He wants no spiritual uplift from you. He wants to touch earth and sky with me. That's a ladylike way of putting it, because you are a lady. Really he wants to fuck. Fuck all day and fuck all night!"

She threw back her head and roared like a young bull. Perhaps seeing me there with my prim expression must have amused her. I banged my fist on the table and asked her what she was laughing at.

She looked at me with tears of mirth in her eyes, sitting

with her feet wide apart and her bare feet with their gold anklets glinting, like her eyes, beneath the army trousers.

"Are you laughing because you can't imagine that José and I have done the same things?" I asked her. "Don't you think José and I also fucked all day?"

"Probably," she replied. "But like I told you before, when it's gone it's gone."

I stayed silent for a moment, allowing her triumph. Her garbled account of your recent history suggested she did not know the full truth. Clearly she did not know the circumstances of why you had joined the army, nor my role in helping you desert. You had not told her about the killing of the foreman. Yet the words, "earth and sky" had been those we used to describe our love. I resented hearing them from her. But the fact that you had not yielded every detail of our own relationship and its origins, suggested that some things clearly remained sacred enough about our love to make you want to preserve it.

I looked at her and wondered whether you were drawn to her in spite of yourself, drawn by the quite involuntary pull of some magnetic force, which I had already sensed on the day of her dance outside the factory. Perhaps, I was prepared to concede, it was neither your fault nor hers, but simply that we are not masters of our own fates.

She, who seemed so much the master of her own, would not hesitate to use astrology and supernatural forces. I guessed she knew how to harness them. Had Carmen bewitched you?

Then she said - unbelievably - "If you join us, you can share José with me."

I felt some compassion for her at that moment. Was this a creature totally devoid of pride or self-interest? I could not believe that she had so little ego. Then I looked at her again, and decided it was pure manipulation. Did Carmen want to get rid of you? Neither her face nor her body language gave any indication of her state of mind.

I did not answer her question.

"I've come here for one purpose only, " I said. "That's to give him a letter. Unlike you, I don't join movements out of love. And although I admire José's beliefs, I represent another class and therefore, can't share them with you."

I walked back to the other room, and realised that I was trembling. You looked up as I came in. It was fear that I saw in your eyes, fear of what she might have told me, and then a spasm of hope. She followed me silently into the room, removing her cap again and twisting her hair up. It was a nervous, repetitive movement, like a tic. Your temporary interest in me evaporated at her entry. You watched her. Your eyes had developed a hunted expression. For the first time I saw how dishevelled you looked. But the life of your eyes was in her face, not in mine. I looked at you with contempt.

Against your impotent silence, Carmen offered me food, a bed for the night. She repeated her offer to me to join and help the movement in any way I wanted. It did not have to be in a military situation, of course.

That was understood. It was impossible to read her. All her words and gestures were edged with manic humour. To everything she said I made no answer. I felt my own spirit ebbing from me.

But equally I felt no compulsion to leave you. I sat at the wooden table, staring down at the dirty floorboards. I saw my own face flatly in the wood. People continued to come and go, some drinking, some not. Some of the men looked at me, but grew bored when I did not return their glances, Then the atmosphere changed. There was a lull which became like a vacuum waiting to be filled.

Then two rather disreputable looking men with pock-marked faces and nervous, darting eyes entered. They had guns slung in holsters and looked identical. They approached Carmen and took her aside. Their expressions were urgent, and they kept glancing around the room, as though afraid of being overheard. I was almost amused by their gung-ho appearance. Carmen listened to what they said without any visible change of expression.

A sense of anticipation flowed from their conversation. Some of the other men muttered that an operation was being planned. And then I heard the sound of hyena laughter coming from two girls I had not seen before, who were eccentrically dressed in bright scarves, bandannas and cheap jewellery.

"Before you go out on that job, Carmen, said the taller of the two, "you should know your fortune."

The girls sat down beside me at the large table and began to cut the Tarot cards. I watched them counting and cutting, sweeping the cards, which had a dark, painterly symbolism, in huge swathes. The girls' loud voices mocked whatever secret missions were being conducted in this place. Yet it was their fortune-telling which distracted me from my own unhappiness. They offered to tell mine. I refused. Some bedrock of Christian morality glimmered through my consciousness and I felt a distant shudder, like an unfriendly hand on my shoulder.

The girls offered the cards to Carmen. For a moment she gestured them away, her mind had turned inward. But I had already seen that she was a creature of changing mood, and so I wasn't surprised when she turned back, with a brief and sad smile. She paused, cocking her head like a woodland animal that has had heard some sound on a frequency too fine for the rest of us, and then murmured: "what the hell!"

She began to cut the cards.

In that moment I met her eyes and we both understood the meaning of her "what the hell." A strange quiet came between us. I felt as though I were being drawn inexorably into her world. Perhaps it came from her half-mocking invitations to join the guerrillas. I realised that she may have offered them as a means of escape for of course it was dangerous to allow someone like myself to discover their hideout and then leave. How stupid I had been, thinking only of my love for you, José! The meaning of my anxiety and the dark premonition I had felt when the two girls began to cut the cards became clear to me.

Since I knew that only death could be the outcome of

this battle of wills between the three of us, I wondered whether hers or mine would be foretold in the cards that day.

Her lips retracted into that grim line. Three times she cut the cards. Three times they told her the same answer.

Nine of Spades. Carmen turned to each one of us in turn, and extended her hands. It was a rather touching appeal, almost a ritual, a rite of passage, an acknowledgement of her perceived fate. Nobody said anything, although another girl at the edge of the room began quietly sobbing. The others all averted their eyes. Carmen's silence was like an indrawn breath. The sense of ritual, of a dark night falling became more tangible, and again I had the uneasy feeling of sacrifice, of something doomed that cannot be saved because of the huge investment of spirit to a greater, insatiable will.

Then without another word, just a thrust of her dark head, she left the room. One of the two girls who had brought in the cards in the first place, screamed and pointed at the ceiling where the biggest cockroach I have ever seen was edging between the cracks.

"Perhaps you should not go on this mission," the other told one of the two grim-faced men. "Carmen has read death in the cards."

For an answer the man cuffed her around the ear.

I went back into her room where I saw the two of you had begun arguing again, this time with a distinct air of fatalism.

"What is it?" I asked you. You shrugged. "She has been seeing evil signs in everything over the last few weeks. Even your coming here. She reads something meaningful into everything she sees. She even swears that the stars have grown bigger and speak to her."

You turned to her in a sudden fury.

"I told you, I'll not have these cards around here any more. They bring nothing but evil. Don't you realise how they infect you and weaken your mind? How do you expect to fight battles when half your mind is turned to jelly?"

And you pulled her towards you from the bed. She was limp and did not resist. You began to shake her.

"What more do you want from life, Carmen?"

"It seems," she smiled wanly, "that life has nothing more to offer me."

"José," I interrupted.

"Yes?"

I waited for a moment before speaking;

"I couldn't tell you before. It's your mother. She is very ill. She talks of you all the time. She's longing to see you but I don't know how much time she has left."

"What do you mean!" you screamed, pulling me towards you. "What do you mean you don't know how much time?"

I was lying. I stammered out some story about her

having had a stroke. I could not stand this deadlock between the two of you. I felt keenly that Carmen was tiring of you and actually sought a freedom that you refused to grant her.

"What do you want me to do?" you asked laconically. I saw then, how you were back in my power, even if just for a moment. Carmen's eyes sharpened when she saw a chance that you might leave her.

"Poor little mother, dying alone, longing for her son. How lucky to have a son to love, whose faithfulness is never questioned. How sad to die alone, feeling betrayed, not by some guy but by the son you reared. Take him with you, Michaela."

"No, no!" you shouted. "I don't believe her. Why didn't she say so before. She's lying!"

I turned towards the door. Oddly, just now I had no feelings for you, José. My lying about your mother had enhanced the sensitivity Carmen felt about her own impending death, as she had foreseen it. She was jealous, not of me, but of the mother dying, perhaps betrayed, but truly, selflessly, loved. She and I, two childless women, had suddenly glimpsed the bitter-sweetness of this incomparable agony.

I turned away because my action, although necessary, made me feel so guilty. And then I heard the snap of castanets and someone slowly picking up the mood on a guitar. Carmen responded with a warm, slow laugh and began to dance with that deep rhythm, throwing back her head, with her teeth bared and her hair flying. The other girls joined in, but further back, away from her, in a respectful distance.

As I reached the door, I felt the room swimming towards me. I put a hand out as though I were falling. Someone grabbed me and guided me away, I don't know where, I have no memory of it, just the room swimming, voices floating, nearer and then further away, and then I no longer felt the pressure of someone supporting me, guiding me. Everything went dark.

CHAPTER SEVENTEEN

The Return

I have come to an empty place. A place of waiting.

Everything passes. Loss. Optimism. But the loss is lit by the optimism and in this flash of inner light I can feel an intangible sense of you, and just as suddenly the sensation is gone and I know that it was always that way; you were nothing more than a fading scent of a flower on a lapel.

I see you now in Carmen's arms. Already you are changed. You wear yourself differently. You have the pinched and folded look of a long-married man. As for me I have to accept this change in you, as I have to accept the passing of love. And I watch you as an old woman mourns the excitement she felt when she was young, when she was with her lover. Yes, I already feel the soured pleasure of one who grows old, who knows she will not experience that intense emotion again but can still remember its taste.

Why should I feel like this when I am still so young?

I grieve because this awareness has come to me as the mountain comes to the long-distance traveller who sees the changing landscape as time melding into space.

I must have fainted while you two were arguing. It was

as though I were drugged. I couldn't rouse myself from a dream that I kept trying to escape from. I dreamed that I ran away from the house. I had the feeling that a strange man with a friendly face I had just met, was a serial killer about to perform experiments on me. I escaped over a back wall. I found myself in my old, familiar streets. The streets I had always known in the waking world. There was a deeply satisfying sense of my parents coming to rescue me. I knew they were coming for me even when I knew that they were not. It didn't matter. In the dream I was saturated with their love and care. My father bent down to kiss me and gently carried me home.

I felt the warmth of his rescue. But I also knew that he did not rescue me. I looked for them. My mother and father. But they were not there. I knew they would never return. I mourned them both with a passion and a vigour that had all the days of my childhood in it but which I could never express in my waking life. In my heart I forgave them. For being who they were. For being wealthy and powerful while others begged and starved. It was not their fault, merely an accident of birth.

I loved them.

In my dream I returned to the house I had lived in all my life which was now surrounded by enemies. I felt the danger like a dark premonition, both here and not yet here. I fell on my knees before the serial killer with the friendly face, and recited a prayer. It was a prayer I had not said since the days the priests vanished in their white robes, chanting and waving their bales of incense, as their robes spun and floated behind them, exciting and scaring me at the same time. They had vanished into history, into my unconscious mind.

The prayer was the Twenty-Third Psalm.

And then I awoke from my stupor to find you gently bending over me. You took my hand and led me out, away from the house of threats and the house of music. I looked around for Carmen, but apart from a burst of laughter, which could have been the snap of a twig, she had disappeared.

After a while the streets of shady commerce disappeared. We were on a country road. Above us a single cloud hung dark and pendulous with rain, yet filtered with light. The cloud leaned over the trees' russet brilliance in a pale reflection of their majesty. There was a damp breeze and the fresh smell of the new season. It held promise. It held sadness. Both were contained in the fullness of the dark cloud outlined by the light. The painterly scene entranced me. You, who knew me so well, smiled and took my hand.

Up till then I had suppressed my emotions, but the touch of your hand brought back all my latent longing for you. In the turn of your head towards me I suddenly saw the young boy who had first captivated me, the stare, the slow smile coming to life, the alert expectancy in your face.

But it was not the same. Now there were layers between us. Layers of otherness. Of Carmen. I had to push them away. You were not the same. And as we walked on, hand in hand, I forgot that I had lied to you. That to my knowledge your mother was perfectly well.

You said: "I hope that you are not using my mother's illness as an excuse to bring me back to you. For you know, Michaela, that I am no longer of you."

I recoiled from these words. It was finished. Once you had said that I was of you and you were of me.

Now I no longer wanted to be Michaela; I wanted to be her, Carmen, to feel these feelings in you for me. I realised also that you were a child of the streets, and it was the venom of the streets that flowed through you now, aroused by her, that she-devil, Carmen.

How would I tell you about your mother? I would say nothing. We would find my car and drive to your village and leave the rest to fate.

I looked at you again critically. "Your mother will find you changed," I said, glancing at your beard. I gently groped with my finger to find the hidden dimple in your chin. You took my hand away.

"My mother will not notice things like that", you said. "She will be glad I'm still alive."

At the traffic lights the street children came running from nowhere, with clowns and puppets, with trinkets and hardware, with yelling and caterwauling. They paused curiously at the car, began touching it, pressing their faces into its red celluloid. Their faces bore the mark of a long life telescoped into a few short years. You stared sullenly ahead.

"I know that you've tricked me, Michaela," you said. "It will do you no good. As soon as I have seen my mother I am going back to Carmen."

❧

It is a fever. I had promised myself a dignified exit, despising those victims of unrequited passion who cling so desperately to their rejecting lovers - yet I found myself begging you, all the way in the car, to come back to me, or at least to let me join you. I, too, would change, would become a freedom-fighter, would renounce my home and throw in my lot with you. You smiled and patted my hair, but at the end of my helpless tirade you took my hand off your knee, put yours over it in a gesture of finality.

"The point is I don't want you to change. You can't change at my pace. It's the pace that alters most in a love affair. That and the differences in peoples' lives. Look at us - you and me. How could it work? I'm a desperado, a deserter, a fugitive. I live on the edge of society and can't re-enter at the place I came in. This is how I will spend the rest of my days. Dodging the army. Dodging the police. You, on the other hand, are a lady. There was always going to be this inequality between us. I could only ever be a plaything to you, Michaela."

"That's not what you used to think. You are my life. You are Carmen's plaything."

"She is a mentor, lover and mother."

"What mother? Mother of the revolution, you mean? You are sick, José. How can you be such a wimp?"

"The best I can hope for is to die with her. Or else to grow old on the streets, like these poor damned children."

"Listen to me, José. I love you and I'm prepared to join you. I share your politics. I love and respect my parents, too, but not what they represent. I am prepared to risk their love for your sake. Can't you see how I am growing, and how much we could share? My education might even be of some use to the revolution, too."

"Do you think I want the intellectual ravings of the educated? Do I want to win your father and his kind onto my side so that we can all sit down and have cosy, theoretical chats based on what you and he understand about oppression? Can't you see that this is the very thing that must be discarded before this country can breathe fresh, unpolluted air again?

"And another thing, all the superstition that comes from the past, all that necromancy and ancestor-worship, it must all go."

"I've just said I am prepared to renounce everything," I said.

But you were not listening.

"Do you know what happens when I go out on a mission with Carmen? We don't talk, we have our maps and our plans. We are prepared and yet ready to act spontaneously when the moment comes. Because in that moment comes freedom - a complete response to the elements and the enemy. So that you know his mood, his eye and his heart. You listen for him. You know he is there, waiting for you. And you know, because you don't listen to your past, to your history - you just act. And you know when the enemy is yours. Just as he knows it. It is beautiful. A merging of souls."

I drove on in silence. We stopped before we reached your village and you changed into the smart clothes I had brought you so you wouldn't be recognised by the police. You had avoided my eyes. How you hated all this. How I hated myself. But then you turned to face me.

"The only reason I have come with you, Michaela," you said, "is because I know that my mother *is* dying. I have sensed it for a long time."

CHAPTER EIGHTEEN

A Love Lost

It was too late. We sat all night in the mausoleum of your room. Your mother lay downstairs under a white sheet, her feet conjoined like a church, her face pulled back towards the earth, flattened, turning to ash before our very eyes. Her mouth was open showing clusters of brown lower teeth, clenching her last moment of life.

"They could have closed her mouth," I observed.

We heard your father sobbing. You kept coiling bits of your jumper around your fingers, twirling and pulling off the wool. You were dry-eyed and silent.

How I longed to speak to her. In her death she was closer to me than you were alive. Had she lived I could have gone on seeing her, preserving my relationship with you even when I knew it was over. A kind of proxy daughter-in-law. But she was dead.

She had died without knowing you were still alive.

"She knew," you said, calmly.

"She didn't know you were still alive."

"She knew but she didn't let on," you said. "Get me some tea, would you? You'll find a kettle in the kitchen."

I could see that you were determined not to allow me any proximity to your mother, even in memory. On the way to the kitchen I stopped to put my arms around your father, who was inconsolable with grief. I was awkward with him. I could not touch his sorrow. It was as though I were not there. Even when I visited your mother, he had hovered in the background, incapable of communication, and I could not reach him now.

"Can I get you something?" I asked him. "I'm bringing José some tea. Would you like some?"

He shook his head. Your poverty drowned out my wealth. It impoverished me, too. I wanted to go out and buy food, lots of it, for this sad and empty house, yet felt impotent to do anything.

"Who will take care of the funeral arrangements?" I whispered, handing you a cup of tea.

You stared ahead of you for a long time. Then you said:

"Now she is dead, my sense of taste has returned."

I sorted out the death certificate with the register office. I took care of the funeral expenses. I stood with the other villagers at the graveside, wearing a headscarf against the dry, desert wind. There was no priest to say a blessing. They lowered your mother into the earth, the wind buffeting the coffin like a ship in a storm. The villagers assembled in two neat furrows to pile on the earth, familiar with it, spading on the red clods as though it were all in a day's work. I left them as you turned to help your father home. There was such a poignancy about the scene in the little churchyard, dwarfed by the low hills and way back by the motionless volcanic mountains, guardians of silent rectitude.

I went home. I was an adult, I decided. I refused to speak of the absent time.

"I am going to paint," I announced to my family. "I don't want to be disturbed all day."

And so I began a period of withdrawal. I wandered the streets and the courtyard of our villa, studying the effect of black on white, shade on sunlight, and most especially, the nocturnal wanderings of my grandmother, who moved through the house with her silent preoccupations.

Stirred, perhaps by your mother's death, I gave full expression to these images of my grandmother. She featured in all my work, either obliquely - walking off the edge of the canvas - or scattered thematically throughout the composition. Bits of her floated from the sky; a profile here, an outstretched arm, there. I painted her in all the ages I could imagine her - young girl, middle-aged and old woman.

But she was the only one who understood that my work was not about her.

She recognised that I was painting *woman*: ageing, traumatised, lonely and ultimately triumphant.

I worked in a monastic silence. Sometimes I heard my mother's heels clip-clopping outside my door, and stopping for a moment. In the past she would have come in and talked. About parties, diplomatic receptions to which we were invited, about situations that had arisen out of petty gossip, about why she was not talking to a particular embassy wife. Now she just paused for a moment or two and went on. It was as though she knew I had been through some kind of trauma and was waiting for me to invite her inside. I did not.

Six months passed in this way. In my studio I was surrounded by huge canvasses, all of them in black and white, until I realised that unless I sold them I would not be able to move, let alone have room to paint.

So I began to hold exhibitions and even won moderate praise. It only intensified my loneliness. I wanted you to be there, to share my success. Six months of artistic activity had not diminished my love for you. The paintings proved to be just another reflection of it. I consoled myself with seeing the events through your eyes. I imagined you sniggering and making snide comments when the national newspaper critics came down like a flock of flamingos, craning their necks to see who else was present at the private view, waiting for their empty glasses to be filled. Bizarre, they called the work. Counter-Expressionist, post Symbolist, proto-neo-Modernist. Etc. etc.

They came to the black and white villa I had built in the grounds of my parents' house. The wittiest among them arrived dressed in black and white, too, as though colluding in some artistic prank. A joke. A ritual. Black and white. What is this madness that grips me? The shadows from the courtyard enhance the monochrome planes of my grandmother. How very beautiful she is; all the intensity of her face shining through the lined flesh. She poses: black dress, black headscarf, face of a white, great beaked bird. Hands in her lap. Their stillness frightens me. They are not a woman's hands. I see a power waiting. The blue veins stand out against the spare, white flesh, taut over the bone, translucent. Not white. Just drained of colour. The long fingers become claws, brown-spotted with age. I don't want to see that they have become predatory. The shadows grow longer. And as I observe her hands I sense the merging of my soul with hers. She can sit here for hours on end without saying a word, not even her breathing has sound; it was she who taught me about the silence within noise, the noise within silence.

Then I looked at her carefully and I saw colours I had never seen before. The deep, brown sadness of her eyes. The grey of her hair made up of the sun's rays and nothing to do with the steel of old hair, and her face, etiolated, yet with the rich hue of earth in it, which is also the colour of decay.

When I first started really looking at her, I was repulsed by her sheer agedness, by the death that stood in her face, by the terror that I would be like that, too, unsaved by love. And then I saw how resistance to love, its overcoming, had sustained her in all her fading colours, and it was at that moment that I stopped thinking black and white and really began to see.

It was the end of the black and white phase between us, too, José.

CHAPTER NINETEEN

The White Pyramid

The guerrilla movement grew stronger. European newspapers headlined the beauty of the oppressed, the dying women and babies, the hopelessness of the street children as though their suffering was the ultimate art form. My family had access to these newspapers, although our local press published nothing about them. It seemed to me that the country was suffering from schizophrenia. I did not know which was the true picture, the screaming headlines of the foreign press, or the familiar acceptance to which I was accustomed, which showed no sudden changes, just a slowly intensifying menace.

As I read about the local terrorist activities I had long imaginary talks with you. I would walk on my own through the red hills. Sometimes I heard the cry of the macaw or spotted some of the brilliantly coloured birds of our region, gathered to take off. There was something awesome, bitter in their flight. They reminded me of novice nuns, hiding their broken hearts behind the veil of chastity.

On one of these lonely walks, it seemed that Carmen appeared to me.

She moved towards me, smiling, welcoming. She held

out her hand as she had done the night she had cut the fated cards. I drew back from this vision of my rival because I felt my jealousy - even of an apparition - as a knife-wound. I remember crying out with actual pain. The next thing I sensed that she was not my rival but my friend. It was almost as though I had become part of her. The jealousy abated, and I was at peace. I felt her speaking from within me.

"Passion is everything in the moment of passion," she was saying, " but it doesn't last, and when it's over it's like the leaf falling from the tree, a natural dissolution of time.

"This is not cruel but reality moving naturally from one element to another, a bee taking its nectar and moving on. Why must you long for attachment? Why can't you accept the true momentum of life? "

These last words I heard as a rustle in trees. But there were no trees, only the sultry, mosquito heat, the intoxicating perfume of the valley and the cry of the macaw.

Strange, this feeling of her, Carmen, the nature child, being inside me, gripping my soul with her pincer-spirit.

Days later she left a telephone message.

"Do you want to see your true country?" she asked. "If so, come to the White Pyramid tomorrow at noon, and you will discover something of interest to you."

Then the phone went dead. I did not know what she meant by the White Pyramid. There were red pyramids and black pyramids, built during the Mayan dynasty. I knew nothing of a white one.

The next day I drove out to the Black Pyramid. The sun moved up behind it and it shone white at me, blinding white so that I had to stop the car. After a few minutes Carmen and José came towards me.

"Open your car door," ordered Carmen. I did so and they piled in, she in the front, he in the back. They told me to drive to a small village in a remote spot in the hills, about 40 kilometres away, that I had not seen for many years.

When we reached it, the place had a sheath of mystery around it, similar to the white, volcanic dust which shrouded Pompeii. I remembered family picnics here as a child. There was a nature reserve, and a monastery surrounded by a formal plantation of trees which welcomed those who sought silence or solace. I used to play among the banana trees while my mother, in a taffeta dress poured tea from a little silver teapot, and unwrapped delicate French pastries from the picnic box.

And something else. Once I had come here to join a party of tourists, hippies and New Age travellers from Seattle, three generations from one family, long-haired and placid, and we had taken donkeys and climbed the mountain beyond the nature reserve. It had taken five hours and at the top the air was filled with the hum of red butterflies which had flown here all the way from Canada to mate and to die.

We had stood like pilgrims, tired and hungry, staring at the whirling vermilion shapes which rose and fell and changed the air, the nature of time and the relationship between ourselves because of their unearthly beauty and their plaintive, almost silent hum.

The memory was peaceful with me. You and Carmen gave me an odd stare, and for a moment I was angry that you had so crudely intruded upon a private dream of the past. You both got out of the car and led the way.

We reached a spot where I saw little houses that looked as though they had been made of baked mud and sand, whose doors creaked as they swung open. You entered one and I followed. There were pots burned to a cinder and a slight smell of gas, suggesting a forced departure. A pair of worn children's shoes, a baby's bottle, the tattered dress of a small girl. The hiss of a dry wind sizzled through the house from far off, spreading like a snake, like the Angel of Death. And the silence became thick and rang in my ears, a distortion of that peaceful hum of butterflies.

I was filled with fear. It was like being slowly turned to ice.

"What happened?" I asked. "This is a ghost town."

You both said nothing. You, José, gently took my arm, and guided me through the village. It was entirely deserted, each house telling the same story of sudden, savage dispersal, leaving nothing.

Suddenly I remembered the village, too. We had walked

its narrow, cobbled streets, had been stared at by its dark-eyed, sombre children. I knew we were different because of the way they had looked at us, and now I remembered the dread with which I had been walked through this village by a father intent on showing me the nether world I must look at but never try to understand, since it would always lie in wait for me with dangerous, hungry eyes.

And I remembered the dread. Because it was here that I understood my privilege, and the fear that such privilege was a loan which carried heavy interest.

I longed to tell someone, but there was nobody who would understand.

Except my grandmother.

"What happened to the inhabitants?" I asked. "Where are they?"

"This is what you should ask the army," Carmen said coldly. "Your army."

"The men of the village were fighting with us, with the guerrillas. The army lined them up to a man and shot them. Then came the women, young girls. Children. They raped them first. Then disembowelled them. They did the pregnant women first. Sometimes, if you come at night, as I do, you can still hear their cries. Most of all I can hear the babies. It was like the days of the Bible, when Pharaoh killed all the first-born Hebrew sons."

I wandered through the town in a daze, alone. You both waited. I tried to imagine faces of people inside the houses, hearing voices, inner voices, laughter, anger, reproof. Not the noises Carmen heard, but the sounds of life being reborn daily in a cycle, and ending without shock or grief or trauma, something that simply happened of its own momentum, while the wind that reached this place from the *tierra caliente*, the hot region, confirmed that beyond the daily current of life lay the desert and the silence, the dry, painless land without memory.

I closed my eyes and shut out those sounds and imagined the place as it once had been, a place of all possibilities, unshaped by human destiny, open to a fierce, godly will. The villagers had taken this space and given it time, a past and present, a future time, too.

And now they were gone. It would be better, much better, I reflected, if the whole place had been simply razed to the ground, if only sand and sky reclaimed it, and that would be not the judgement of history, just the continuum of empty space with the spirit of the Creator singing through it and the hand of the Creator sifting sand. Better. Kinder.

I had reached the car now. You were standing there, watching me. I thought of Carmen as she had appeared to me in my imagination. As a nature spirit. Yes, she had said she walked here at night sometimes. But now she was different. A hard-faced woman carrying a rifle. She called the shots. She had a head full of phrases. The dialectics of dissent. A dictionary of political assertions. And you. Like her shadow.

I did not want your politics. They were irrelevant now. Tasteless. I was repulsed by them. You had created a scene for me, fixed the set, the sound, lights and cameras.

I was walking towards you. My anger seethed. It was not against the perpetrators of these crimes. It was against you.

I was determined now. She would not have you. I would win you back. You were watching me. Two people with the eyes of one. I ignored you. Cold as ice I stepped back into the driving seat. I was in control, just as I had been on the day I looked properly into my grandmother's face and saw who I was and what I had come from.

"You have nothing to say," said Carmen. " Words fail you, don't they? This is what they, your people, have done. And there are more villages like this one. Burnt-out skeletons of homes."

She was about to get into the seat beside me, but you pulled her back.

"Shut up!" you said. "Don't tell her what to feel. Leave her alone."

Then she put her arms around you and began to kiss you, coldly, with that precise intent in her eyes. You responded, but with a dry passion and pulled her towards you. She came to you like an animal,

I watched it all from the car, frozen and impassive, mesmerised at the brute harmony of your love which I knew was not love, not our love, and I saw its difference and the way it united you. And then I knew I had to break this unity and I got out of the door and brushed you aside, and what stopped you was when you saw that I, too, was naked, and then all the tenderness returned to you, and Carmen picked me up with her small, solid strength and carried me with a gentleness she imbibed from you, and so gentle, so like a grandmother who has seen the earth beneath the flesh, she lay me in her lap and you cupped my face in your hands and kissed me with the clenched mouth of your brutality, while she fondled me and allowed you to enter me, and I loved it, the brutality that pierced the tenderness that made me own you and then I pushed you away and made love to her, to her because it was the only way, and she was neither woman nor man to me, but the brutish extension of you that I had to destroy, because this was how you saw it, and this was how you wanted it, and so I loved her, knowing now that she must die.

CHAPTER TWENTY

Revenge

So it happened. I was of you and her. The former Michaela was torn out, eradicated. Michaela did not exist. And I became the world of beggars.

People watched me, whispering, pointing, as I wandered the streets with bags of money, wandered among the dirty beggar children whose faces seemed to grow poorer, thinner, each day. I, on the other hand, rattled, clanked with money. And I wanted to be rid of it.

No longer Michaela of the black and white villa and the arty parties. Moneybags Michaela, the painter gone finally mad.

First they stared and then they swooped. Little birds of prey, they were, and I was their scarecrow, letting them whoop and guffaw around me, emptying my pockets, as I smelled the rank stench of their dirty clothes, their unwashed bodies, the graveyard smell that rose from their foul, doomed youthfulness.

I allowed them. I became a lump of wood. I let them strip me of jewellery. I let them tear at my clothes. I let them. And this was how I came to be ragged like them. Physically as well as emotionally I came to share their grief. As I was part of you, part of Carmen, so I wanted to be part of them, have them be part of me. It seemed the only way.

Lovers passed me. A tall, black American tightly holding a sapling of a young girl, bending her to him so that she walked lop-sided. I heard disjointed snatches of their conversation.

"If anyone so much as dares to look at you, I'll break every bone in his body."

They vanished, blossom quivering in the air. A faint reminder of what had been.

The children vanished, too. Once it had been necessary to push them off, but now they disappeared with their rasping street-rap songs, having exhausted every possibility I offered them, having used me up, sucked me dry.

I looked up, exhausted. Far away in the hills I saw a column of smoke rising from the local power station. It gave me the feeling of something very old, very poignant and symbolic, like pipe-smoke unfurling from an Indian village, speaking peace, speaking war. There were memories here, subtle and darting, that made me gasp and force back tears. Old memories of safe times from a deluded childhood. The fresh, pungent smell of cut grass now rose in my nostrils, separating earth from sky.

But the earth was rotten and I was part of that rottenness. The old, safe memories fused with the newer, more exciting memories of our love, making the pain exquisite, unbearable. I lay down and must have fallen asleep.

They found me in the fields. A string of rare pearls which the beggar children could not tear off my neck broke after they ran away. I was lying bedraggled among the pearls.

My father lifted me up. The others, peering behind him, thought I was in a trance or a coma. I saw myself as though from above, from outside my body, my eyes staring vacantly at the skies. My father could not look at my face. His own was torn between grief and anger. It was the first time I had seen any such look on his face.

A deputation from the village was coming towards us. Complaining about the government's latest repressive measures against the insurgents, which would affect them, even though they were innocent, about a newly imposed curfew. My father continued walking. The villagers came, waving banners, yelling insults, shaking their fists. They came armed with pickaxes and crude, farm implements. They shouted at us. Their shouts were like a great whale heaving towards us. My father continued to ignore them. Someone came right up to us and held a scythe up to my father's face. He paused for just one minute. Death, I thought. Symbol of death. I could see the black hairs inside the man's dilated nostrils. My father moved on, his face devoid of expression. Eventually they cleaved a path for us to walk along, my father carrying me, my mother, complaining now about her shoes which pinched her, and the rest of the family behind. The insults died down. An uneasy silence hovered over the villagers as they began to withdraw in a tide of slow frustration.

My father carried me through the streets. Baleful lights

shone between the broken shutters which creaked menacingly in the light wind. Immobility helped me to see clearly. I saw you between the shutters, planting bombs; their eyes were your eyes, yours and hers. You could not understand my lethargy. Everything must have the name of action, you said.

The streets bubbled with silent hostility. Anger, vengeance, sang behind the windows.

And I saw my father's courage for the first time. His daughter had become a street beggar, victim of street beggars. The thought occurred to me that in such times, in such shame, he could have left me for dead or finished me off with the revolver he always kept in his desk drawer. No questions would be asked of the oligarchy.

But he did not. He picked me up, like the normal father I had never known, and carried me home. It came to me that he was suffering, too. The villagers' insults, threats and anguish had rained on him, too, but this was merely the overture to what lay in wait. And he – head of the household – was as vulnerable as they were.

Perhaps it was a gesture of defiance or perhaps the first statement of surrender. See here, he was saying. We are all equal. Accept my shame for your shame. Here is my hand. Yet there were no takers. The air was swollen with an angry, foetid wind that would not rage, clouds that would not burst. The humidity clung to us. When we reached home I was soaked through with it and with the sweat of my fear.

Though my lips would not speak and my eyes felt as

though I were peering through fine muslin I saw the grim whiteness of my mother's face as she leaned over me. My brother's face was contorted with rage.

"She has brought nothing but shame on all of us and on the name of the family," he shouted hysterically to my father.

"This José, for whom she is quite prepared to destroy herself, is a terrorist who will bring us all down," said my mother.

"And we gave him sanctuary! He'd stop at nothing. One day he will kill us all."

My father turned to them both in appeal. Though I could not move, I could see him grown helpless, like a child, under the steel of their bitterness. This man, my father, with his airs and graces, his very scent of groomed and finely-honed power, now raised his hands, as though to placate his wife, caress her in her hysteria, but she moved away and slammed the door in his face.

Then he turned to me.

"Where is he? This José of yours? Tell me where I can find him!"

"No. Never!"

"Tell us – or you will regret it!" shouted Alvarez.

"No! Not if I die! Not if you kill me!"

Suddenly my father's eyes grew hard. He tore at his hands, helplessly, furiously, looked away, stared at me again, threw up his hands in despair.

"Leave us," he told my brother. And when he had reluctantly closed the door behind him. "You know that I can turn you over to the police?"

From somewhere I replied calmly: "You must do whatever you must."

Then with a groan I had never heard from him, my father began swearing at me, pummelling me with his fists, lashing at me with his hands in a passion of rage, love and hate. I would not cry out or beg him to stop. And only with the last blow, he whimpered, more like a child than a father, begging my forgiveness. I looked at him silently, through swollen eyes.

At last he collapsed, exhausted beside me, sobbing, all his anger quenched, holding me, bruised and bleeding in his arms. I felt a glimmer of remorse and compassion for them in the game that was forced on them by fate to play. And because in all his savagery he was nearer to me than my mother, who had showered me with finery as he had with blows, and nearer to me than you, who had betrayed me.

CHAPTER TWENTY-ONE

The Lovers

The burglars came in silence, thieves of the night, opening drawers, and cupboards, taking silver, jewellery and money, disappearing before dawn.

No-one heard them. Nobody knew about it until the servants rose to begin their chores and then a long wail sounded through the house as the wreckage of the rooms was discovered. The police came. The servants lined up to be finger-printed. But we knew the thieves came from the village.

"You see what all your good deeds have done!" My father reproved me. But there was no evidence. Despite extensive searches none of the valuables was ever found. It gave me an eerie sense as I walked through the house. Our invincibility had been violated. It changed us. We felt unsafe, I in my little black and white villa, they in their mansion.

"What we need is something to look forward to," said my mother when the fuss died down. "Like a wedding."

"Don't look at me," I said to her. "I am the youngest child. You still have Alma and Alvarez."

"But you are the most successful."

"It's not the time for weddings, mother," I told her.

In the following weeks, despite my protests, the courtyard was filled with suitors, would-be lovers. They came in droves, as though I were a circus attraction. I locked myself in my house, but they banged on the shutters. When I saw them I became furious. I brought out a whip and cracked it on the hard marble of the courtyard paving until sparks of electricity rose, and they shimmied away in fear.

"Imbeciles!" I called after them. "What makes you think I would marry any one of you?"

Their tactics became more subtle. They telephoned, giving false names. Their voices were the assorted voices of lovers; commanding, mellifluous, rounding the vowels of my name into a caress.

Micha-e-ela. Micha-e-la. They coil around me like snakes. Of course: I represent big money; an empire, a rite of passage through a land where everything else is crumbling. Can I blame them for trying? For how long, anyway can we retain this power over the masses?

My parents and brother argue and debate over it. They no longer bother to send the servants away. I see the house falling to decay. Since the night of the burglary my mother has lost her talent for preservation. Every day another precious vase breaks, sometimes falling to the floor of its own volition. A dead bird appears on the courtyard floor with a fatal knife-wound to the throat, but no evidence of attack. Our empire has become like Rome in its last days, where dead animals, minus essential organs, foretold disaster as white-robed senators hurried nervously to the forum.

Sometimes I see my father standing in the sunlight. His hair, his forehead and his eyes are clear as ever, but the rest of his face is shrouded in a kind of mist. It is a recurring image. I read it as a bad omen.

The poor now keep silent vigil in the streets, no longer selling, hustling, grafting, just staring, their eyes as empty as their bellies. It is as though all that's left is the waiting. I stare back at them from my window. I am afraid, afraid also that I have no feelings left.

My father continues to make important phone calls around the world, his hair is greying now and his quilted dressing gown has grown shabby, his voice, too, has developed a piercing sound when he becomes excited, but nobody notices.

Nothing feels the same. It is like a spiritual earthquake, the ground cracking and sighing beneath me. I think of that night when we were together, you, me, Carmen. Are we all corrupted by that sin?

And yet it did not feel like a sin. It couldn't have been another way. Carmen, José. And Michaela. The corruption, on the other hand, feels genuine. I sense destructive forces all around me. I wake up dry-mouthed, tension in the pit of my stomach. The silence beyond the daily noises of the house, the domestic noises, is like a cavern, calling me into its depths, warning me that the life I knew has morphed into another life. Telling me that everything has changed.

"I am Pedro," said the man who appeared in the court-yard as I set up my easel to catch the morning light.

"Do you want to be my lover, too?" I asked him in a bored, flat voice, without even bothering to glance at him.

"No, for you have no need of lovers," he replied. "Those you have rejected are now sitting with the poor in the streets. You bring no happiness to any man, Michaela."

"Well, what do you want then?"

"I have come to replace your grandmother."

I looked at him. He wore jeans and a corduroy jacket with an open-necked shirt. An ordinary man. Neither poor nor wealthy, neither ugly nor handsome.

But there was something lean and compelling about him.

He stood there, leaning against a bougainvillaea bush, one leg behind the other, the shadows playing against the sharp contrast of his features. As I looked at him he became so unusual that I started to paint him, and I painted him all day, filling canvas after canvas with him. I began by painting him in great detail, down almost to the last quiver of hair on his moustache, but by the time I had finished all my artistic experiments I had reduced him to a simple black rose on a white canvas. It was then that I realised that I had not needed to look at him at all, for something in his essence had suggested the tragic lyricism of the black rose. But as I looked up he had gone. I felt a sense of dread. The black rose seemed to step out of the canvas. What could it mean? A rose. Romance. But black. Black romance? He had come to replace my grandmother, he said. He was a madman. What did he mean?

And then a terrible, cold feeling went through me. I began to run for my grandmother, calling her name through the empty house, for the servants had gone, and the house merely echoed with my cries, throwing her name back into my face.

When I found her lying peacefully on her bed, her face had developed the serenity that I had foreseen in my paintings. I held her close to me and sobbed.

They played the Fate Theme at my grandmother's funeral. It had been requested in her will. The wealthiest and most powerful families of the land gathered, from the President downwards. They sat in prim lines against the walls of our long, Victorian-arched conservatory, talking in whispers. From somewhere, my mother, who usually clattered about in stiletto heels, just to sound decisive, just to prove her status, had developed the silent footsteps of my grandmother. She glided through the house, offering mint tea and tortillas, a smile of other-worldly peace on her face, almost as though her raging soul had been assuaged by the death of her husband's mother.

The VIPs sat, vacuum-packed in their black suits, solemnly eating and drinking, filling the familiar atmosphere with their unfamiliar presences, their imposed mourning silence. But there was no silence in me. Inwardly I was screaming. I was screaming for this grandmother who had taken the pacific mystery of old age to the grave, dragging with her, like a long train, all the years of my childhood. One of the black figures stood up suddenly and stretched, in the grip of a yawn, teeth bared, leering. He cast a long, dark shadow against the sunlight. It was the signal to break the stillness. Now the mourners began to move, to mix and talk to each other. They were no longer one uniform, dark shape. They turned into people, separate, expressive, without harmony. There were couples among them who argued, who didn't like each other. And inevitably some of them broke into me, into my bitter thoughts, bringing their darkness to mingle with mine. I could not face it. I started to retreat from them. I saw the woman with a twisted smile who would engage me in crippling conversation.

Already she was moving towards me, mouthing false condolences. I looked around for an escape route, but my way was blocked. Suddenly I did not care what she thought. I did not care about manners. My grandmother had died and I was entitled to behave badly. I pushed past the crowds and cut off her approach, leaving her to find another victim.

From the hall I could hear a piano being played in my sister's room upstairs. The music evoked feelings I'd had as a child returning home and seeing the soft movement of her curtain in the upstairs window. I realised that it had always made me feel glad, that faint floral imprint of the curtain through the lining, snatched by the sun. It had been reassuring, a small continuum, a knowledge of myself linked to this sister, this speechless sister, in her amniotic sac of music.

I went upstairs now and entered her room. What my sister did never surprised anybody. The fact that our grandmother lay in her coffin downstairs while she played Chopin in her room was normal. She looked up at me now, the music deep under her fingers, and then she stopped playing. She waited, looking down at the keyboard.

"What is grief?" I asked her. "I cry all night long for him. I can't stop, somehow. It's like a convulsion. Maybe that's what grief is. A convulsion of life. Maybe you cry, too? Do you? I'm sure you do."

I looked at her. Her face was in shadow. She was very still. One finger began to trace the outline of the C major key.

Impulsively I placed my hand over hers. The pressure made the keys reverberate through the room. She turned her face away from me and I felt a twinge of remorse.

"Of course", I said quietly. "*These* are your tears, aren't they?"

For the first time I was longing to tell her what happened. But I decided to say nothing. Not to tell her about what had happened to me. Nor about the letters I had received from Carmen.

They took the coffin like a piece of meat on a skewer and lowered it into the grave. And my mind drifted to your mother's funeral. We had stood together that day, among the villagers. Despite the sadness of the occasion, I had experienced that lightness of being, that sense of the universe opening out for us that came whenever I saw you. Now I felt a terrible emptiness, an anger, that you were not beside me.

My father had hired a full male choir to sing his mother to her final rest. Their voices rose like the swoop of a bird, upwards through the air. Although I found their presence distasteful, the masculine warmth of the sound thrilled me. I stood with closed eyes, hair drawn back, feeling the sun edge through the corners of my dark glasses. The choir became one voice, now deep, yet transcendent. I tried not to cry. I felt guilty that I was thinking more of you than my grandmother.

CHAPTER TWENTY-TWO

Wrestling With Angels

She came to me, as I knew she would. At first with letters. Cajoling, persuasive. Later with dreams. And still later, with presences. Whispering, mocking me. Dancing in the rain, in the wind which hurled itself against the windows in the stormy season, curtains swirling. I would glimpse her eyes in a flower in the wallpaper, and hear her laughter in the creak of a door. I would come into my room and imagine her sitting on the bed. She'd stand up and click her hands as though they were castanets and begin to dance provocatively around me, so that I could feel the caress of her black hair on my neck, the smell of her perfume, the sense of a street electrified by her presence. And I would be exhilarated by the thought of dancing with ghosts. "You are almost there," her voice would whisper. "Your true being is telling you where you are. We were so close, that night on the mountain, three spirits fused into one. You don't belong there, in that great white house where you were born. Just because you are born into a family, into a class system, doesn't mean you belong there. You belong with us. Leave them. Join us. It is not so difficult. You can change. Have courage, Michaela. Have courage. We are waiting for you, José and I."

And she lingered in my imagination. When I walked

through the corridors of my house, her perfume would be there. That keen blend of human grace with the raw quality of animals. What hold did she have on me? I was vulnerable to her spirit because of what had happened on the mountain. And I longed for surrender into friendship just to get rid of this tension. If the tension would pass between us, I could put my head on her shoulder, ask her advice, plead for safety, for assurance, without some impending sense of doom, of threat by her spirit towards mine.

"You have already fallen," I could hear her whisper. "What are you waiting for, now? Just leap. That's all it takes. Leap into the abyss with us." It came to me that Carmen was always in my thoughts, whether I tossed and turned, sleepless in bed, or whether I felt her in the cloudy silence of the mountains. And then I would suddenly push her away like someone awakening from dream. What was I thinking of? Why was I obsessed with her when all that mattered was you? You wrote me this letter.

My dear Michaela, I know that you are waiting for a sign from me. I have been unable to make any gestures either of friendship or love. You see me as a man under a spell. Do forgive me. It is my hunger that speaks. There is a throb in this land which must be heard, which cries out for justice. It is the throb of pain, indifference, isolation. My hunger for Carmen is my hunger for this justice. I hear that you are painting now, and some would say your work is subversive. Good. I am glad that you have learned something from the experience with us, even though your path may be different.

Of course, I know you couldn't come with me. I think you can fight on your own without guns. Our tragedy is that together we can't harmonise these two spheres. I saw that many times in your parents' house and I didn't want to believe it at the time. This was what drove me to drink. I am happy, in a way. No-one has complete happiness. But we must be honest with one another and it would be a lie to pretend that my feelings for Carmen are dying. Our time together, you and me, was right then, but not now. You guided me through my first adventure with battle; the death of the foreman made me realise that I couldn't neglect my social responsibilities for ever, wearing the uniform of a soldier in our army while that same army sanctioned the right of a foreman to rob my parents and enslave them to their own land.

You saved my life, Michaela, and more important, my spirit. Through you, I have come to see the ethic to which my life must now be dedicated. My relationship with Carmen is more dangerous. She has many lovers and little patience. It makes me very jealous. It destroys my own integrity. But as the leader of our cell she has responsibilities and mood swings. Don't imagine that I love her more than you. My love for you has not changed, only its timing. Please don't agonise over my failure to send you an address. You must understand that I am in great danger. I can't let you share that danger with me.

My love always, José

I tore up the letter in a fury. How dare you be so patronising! How dare you claim ownership of my life and my art! And yet a wave of tenderness came over me. I thought how beautiful it had been when our love was just in the air between us, not yet in the flesh. Made flesh it became destructive. But it was of her that I dreamed, and not of you. My house, my black and white house, became full of her. The one night she did not come to me was the night I put the pillow over my head and swallowed enough sleeping pills to ensure a night's oblivion. In that night I dreamed I was drowning. I felt the warm water lapping over me. Not unfriendly - whispering and lapping. We have come to take you, it whispered. Let us take you down, down, down. And I allowed the waves to swallow me. It felt so natural, beautiful, peaceable, for all the rushing of the waves was above, on top of me, filling my ears with love and enticement, and below was the peace, the sad, sweet peace of dreams.

If I allowed it. But I did not. I began to struggle. I began to fight the waves and the storm for all the friction of life above. I could feel the salt of the water clogging my nostrils, clamming my throat. And I felt then that I could not evaporate, I could not pass away into the peace. And I also felt that it was not possible that the universe could shut down on me like that. That my one fractured vision could be clouded over and eliminated, destroying the world with the closing of my own consciousness.

But in spite of your desire to remain hidden, in spite of the dangers you spoke of, you and Carmen became respectable.

You were seen together at diplomatic receptions. You mingled with well-known personalities, spoke earnestly about the important issues facing our country. You even fronted charities for the poor.

My friends who sat over endless cups of coffee in the Glass Houses, spoke of the mystery woman who had captivated many prominent statesmen; she had been spotted with them in celebrity night-clubs, her eyes always hard as steel, seeking the main chance.

Or so they perceived her.

One moment she was a foreign spy or a political journalist, the next a high-class whore who took pleasure in education. They described you as a tall, handsome, silent man in dark glasses never far from her side, watching her. A minder.

But they spoke from a political lassitude, almost a helplessness which began to affect many people. I sensed it everywhere - this lull between an end and a beginning. It created an urge to party, to lavish hospitality, to speak of stocks and shares, to take refuge in bland talk of the higher investment the USA was planning to make into the Central American economy. And yet in the pauses, you could sense the fear of something that hung in the air, something threatening that could not be defined. The women - particularly keyed in to the subtleties of imminent change - were concerned about their children. This was what stimulated an incredible need for glamour. With an almost fatalistic insouciance the ruling families turned their attention inwards, to decorating their houses in the most exotic and lavish styles, with what I can only describe as a fin-de-siècle decadence. The women at this time had never appeared more expensively dressed. Street poverty was buried beneath a glut of designer labels that thronged the pavements and patios and the Glass Houses, and the more glamour that appeared on the outside, the duller, the shallower was the mental and emotional state within. Nobody, it seemed, could concentrate on a serious matter for more than a few minutes.

Into this unbalanced state of affairs, two newcomers, emerging like aliens from another planet, with neither history nor future but plenty of opinions, provided an exotic relief.

It was almost a national rescue attempt.

At a diplomatic reception given by the US ambassador, I bumped into you. You barely noticed me. I nudged the ambassador and asked him about you. Who are they? I demanded. But I received no clear answer. He smiled urbanely, almost as though no respectable party could take place without them. Your eyes were never far from each other. You touched without touching. I saw her mocking smile, and you hovered - anxious but out of reach - generating a buzz of exotic entertainment.

For some reason I pushed it further.

"Do you really know who they are? Have they been properly vetted by Security?" I asked the ambassador. He laughed and said, yes, they are people to be watched, but they certainly help to make a party go with a swing. And he himself was already loutish with drink, clinging to a noisy blonde girl of about 17.

I realised with bitterness that your letter only had an abstract meaning. In the flesh I aroused nothing in you any more.

A small group of people attached themselves to you,

drawn to that charisma you both evinced of being entirely different from anyone else. I overheard you speaking, somewhat riskily, about the need to take responsibility for the poor. Your work in the streets was supported by the International Red Cross, you told one bejewelled old lady, whose skin wobbled like a Tudor ruff around her bull neck. It was high time the ruling families stopped patronising the poor and actually did something to relieve their misery.

There was the odd murmur of animosity but you looked so inexplicably well-dressed and Carmen so elegant that no-one took real exception. Most of your audience betrayed the pleasure the ruling class takes in being upbraided for their excesses.

Later you were to chuckle cynically at the way the aristocracy could be so fooled by you, not even attempting to uncover your true origins, let alone grasping the sentiment behind the radical words. As for me, it was difficult to keep my mind on what you said because of the fire of my emotions. The glass in my hand shook and my conversation with people who came up to me grew disjointed.

Later that night, as we went for dinner into one of the embassy's grand, presidential rooms for state or ceremonial occasions, I sensed Carmen behind me. Her bronzed hand was on my arm, in an almost possessive gesture.

And suddenly an intense feeling of remorse came over me for the frailty I glimpsed in her for the first time. I remembered her cutting the cards which predicted her destiny. For a moment she no longer radiated that mocking humour but the peace of acceptance. It was as though another Carmen walked with her, a purer, more abstract being.

But I was not the only one touched by the peculiar poignancy of Carmen that night. The US First Secretary, a tall, walrus-eyed man with a permanently sour expression due to his constant failure to navigate the seas of lust, could not take his eyes off her all evening. He was quite glued to her, murmuring into her ear, gazing meaningfully into her eyes as he refilled her glass, oblivious to your raging jealousy. This time, he was sure, Lady Luck would be with him.

This man became known to us as the Bullfighter because of the impossible battles he took on in dealing with foreign governments, though in this respect fate rewarded him rather better than it did his amorous adventures. He saw in the beautiful Indian woman, not another romance doomed to failure, but a foreign enterprise which must be handled with skill and extreme subtlety. In her company his face, began to lose its habitual sourness and betrayed the sheer pleasure of the hunter.

I left the party in a mood of deep depression. I thought of the days of the week marshalled around me like a guard of honour, each with its own destiny. Monday through to Sunday. Another function for each day and a sense of the world never pausing, yielding nothing to me.

Carmen's happiness, on the other hand, seemed complete.

The Bullfighter took her everywhere. Their pictures appeared in the social columns of all the newspapers. Once he flew her out to New York and they appeared together on a political chat show. She was groomed and sleek as an American film star. It is her feet I remember from the news photos. Sturdy and well apart in a pair of red high-heeled shoes. You could see the tendons prominently because of her dancing. Her shoulder muscles stood out, too, in photographs where she was shown gathering the poor children to her with one arm, the other holding a bouquet of red flowers. Her red lips gleamed.

She had achieved her wish. She had become an icon.

You wrote to me about The Bullfighter. I didn't want to hear it. I don't want to be your mother or your sister. Leave me out of it – I wanted to reply. At night, demons rocked my sleep; they sat with arched thighs like bridges at the foot of my bed. Grinning. Digging needle-sharp nails into my anger and stirring, stirring.

I read your letter in many different ways. I read it on the hot streets, away from the grand house of solitude where my family had grown into disparate beings leading separate lives, and reading it made me aware of how events had changed me.

Michaela,

The last thing I want to do is to burden you, but I'm losing my reason and desperately need your advice. This woman is mad. Mad and bad. She is our common enemy. Up till now I have tolerated her mood swings and flirtations, but this latest lover is more dangerous. Perhaps she is using him to help us, to win him over to our side, ridiculous as this may seem, but even so I utterly reject that – as I reject his very being.

We had so much need of each other in our common cause, and suddenly she falls in love. In love she calls it! With an outsider, too. This man has utterly seduced her. She has totally abandoned our work. One night I lay in wait for him and pounced on him. I only meant to give him a few punches, to teach him a lesson but something goaded me on and I couldn't stop hitting and kicking him, even when he lay on the ground begging for mercy, the fucking coward. I could hear myself screaming at him, as though the words were coming out of a different mouth, telling him that I would rearrange his face for him, but at that moment Carmen turned up and hauled me off him. She went ice-cold and silent. She refused to speak to me, and in fact now she has disappeared. I had no idea where she was until I saw her picture in the papers. Her and that bastard. I can't accept that things are over between us. Even worse I can't stand the person I have become, full of hatred.

I will do something desperate, I know. Please write.

Your José.

My José! Even wandering alone in this city offers no protection from you nor from the callousness of your words. Your violence has infected me, too. I see threats and anger everywhere, and most clearly the bitter state of my soul.

But there is a killer instinct rising within me. Every night I fight the devils, crying out to them to leave me alone. And still they come. The demons have led me to this place. I wrestle and wrestle with them and at the end I do not know whether they are demons or angels. I know that action must follow their defeat.

Some nights I hear your voice calling to me for help, and when I reach out I can almost touch you.

But after this letter I heard nothing from you for three weeks.

CHAPTER TWENTY-THREE

Unto Death

I awoke staring up at the atrium through which the sun bore down like a wild animal trying to force its way in. Two words - Unto Death - came to mind. I could hear them in some imaginary priestly enunciation, but did not know whether they referred to the commitment of love as in the marriage vows or to some battle-to-the-death. Unto or until Death - I couldn't be sure, and it bothered me which it was, but suddenly I remembered my grandfather and the smell of peppermint seemed to fill the room. He had so loved the taste of menthol mints that he had them especially imported from England.

I picked up a photograph of him taken with my grandmother on their wedding day. Until death did them part. It was one in which his mouth was open as though he were about to burst into laughter. I kept staring and squinting at it, willing that smile to energize into the sound of real laughter for me, willing them both to come to life here in the room with me, to console me with their kindness. But in my mind now I could only see their dead, parched faces, their frozen grimaces, as I had seen them in their coffins.

As the menthol smell wafted away I was filled with a sudden longing for the years which had passed in the time of my obsession with you. I had celebrated my 18th birthday four years ago and late into the night, after the guests had gone home, I had stayed up watching old video films of my childhood, which I used to watch with my grandfather. I remembered him putting up the old white screen, darkening the room, and feeling the excitement I had always felt of the past sliding into the present on a dusty beam of light from the 8 mm camera. I mourned the chattering creature who had become this fractured teenager and recognized that the essence of childhood is perhaps the only true essence we shall ever have before the bodies of disaffection, anguish, ambition and enchantment, fall upon us like carrion birds to eat away our true selves.

Unto death. Till death us do part. But maybe I am wrong. Why should I imagine that a love affair must last for ever?

There is someone knocking softly at the door. I get up, pull on my dressing gown, shake down my hair. Wait, wait, I shout. I am coming.

I catch my breath. You are standing at the door

"I am sorry", you say. "Probably I shouldn't have ..."

"Don't be silly, don't be silly."

Something bitter spreads inside me as I lead you inside. Some gut warning. We sit on the bed. The euphoria goes from me. Your stance is caring, romantic, but I know that you are lying. In your body you are lying. Your soul is elsewhere.

Yet you take my hand and for a moment there is an

elision of hope between us because you are looking at me and speaking to me as you did in our first days. But I can't trust this hope.

And I say to you, lightly, tactlessly - have you been drinking this early? You ignore that and run your hands delicately through the strands of my hair, so that I can see you mourning me, wishing things had been otherwise. This is too painful, and I push your hand away. Then you sigh, and look down at your hands in your lap on which I see two rings, one mine the other hers.

"I am in the grip of some madness," you say.

"The drink has addled your brain," I reply tersely.

"I don't drink any more. It's her. She's an evil spirit," you say.

"Evil she is not. She is many things, but not evil. No. It's the political thing she represents that has got you, that has made you so susceptible. An accident waiting to happen, perhaps?"

You ignored my glib tone.

"Won't you help me? I'm shit scared. I've rehearsed this many times, Michaela - what I would say to you. Regrets, sorry, take me back. That sort of thing. The truth is a bit less than that. I do still love you. But I feel the danger from my own self. With you, I'd feel ..."

"Protected?," I say.

"Yes. From what I might do."

"What will you do, José?"

You don't answer.

Then, after a moment:

"Without you my life is ruined."

"If fear is stronger than love, José, then yes, it is ruined."

"Then help me to strengthen it again. To make it what it once was."

You went on with confused explanations. Emotional contrivances. We were like a married couple, you said. There was a measure of peace between us. Until, I said bitterly.

Yes, until.

I had meant your self-destructive spirit. You didn't see it that way.

Until her, you said.

No. I insisted. Until you.

I was wife and she was mistress, you said. She had one extra gift. She saw you less and perceived you more. Romantic self-indulgence, I snorted. And now?

"It's too late, José."

How horrible these words. Horrible. To try to explain the way love embraces and then slides away.

You reach for my hand again. Yes, I see now how my feelings would die if left to dwindle naturally, unaided by this power of romantic memory. I feel a flicker of disgust as I look at you, for the way you betrayed me, for the way your alcoholism seeped into your flesh and finally your spirit, which became flimsy as a tissue in her hands.

And I felt disgust, too, for these repetitive post-mortems into our affair.

No. It could never be the same again.

But, on the other hand I could help you. I could lead you away from malign influence. And what would be left between us? We would become brother and sister. Full of platitudes. And sometimes harsh words would rise up to level us, to discharge the dying emotions of which we would no longer speak. Love in diminuendo.

The death of love.

"No," I said.

Gently and sadly, then, you took my face in your hands and your kiss confirmed the passing of our love. I cradled your head in my arms as you wept, and it was as though you were somewhere else, looking down on me and that I was comforting our child. I heard a deep sigh passing through you. Your head, fallen to your chest, had a premature aspect of greyness I feared you may not live to achieve. I noticed that the fringes of the small, Turkish carpet beside my bed were ruffled, and it irritated me that I couldn't stand up and shake them out. It irritated me more that I could think about such mundane things at such a time. But perhaps it helped me.

"Go now, " I said softly, "while my back is turned. Don't

let me see your face, as you go."

Through the window I hear the idle chatter of the gardeners. I concentrate on them and so blank out the sound of the door closing behind you. It seems I will always hear them.

I remained standing beside the bed for a long time, allowing the awareness that something important had taken place to sink in. After a few moments I could feel again. I thought of your leaving me in the morning, the dull day lifting, lightening, like a child unwillingly born, the symbol of long, empty years ahead.

Unto death.

In some deep crevice where no-one can enter, I am crying. If madness is not a state but a place where it is impossible to touch, make contact, then I am in it. The zone where no-one hears me cry. People who suffer this peculiar madness, this misaligned gift of extended perception, may notice others exchange looks with one another, but never with them. They alone, the mad ones, believe they understand the true use of eyes and language.

At night the demons return. Often they take her form. At other times my own. I have stared up at my own face hovering above me, made ugly with jealousy and frustration. My face disappears and changes into hers. We wear many disguises. Sometimes I wear the coned hat of a victim of the Spanish Inquisition, prepared to die at the stake. Sometimes I am a crusader, killing for

Christ. I have seen myself indulge in excesses of lust and sadism beyond my own imagination. Love and cruelty intermingle to the point where I can't tell the difference between them. Then the devils disperse, and I see a procession of nuns and monks chanting. Their chant fills the air, a perfect syncopation of breath and harmony, until the harmony dissolves into the sound of inhalation and exhalation, which itself becomes the breath of the sea. I become aware of a blue light, of the presence of God, both in the time of my goodness and the time of my evil.

Carmen has a new apartment in the consular district. I wait there from the first light of each day, between the eucalyptus trees, watching those who come and go. When she goes out I follow. Sometimes on foot, sometimes in my car.

I stalk my prey.

Today I am standing behind a queue of chattering schoolchildren in a sweet-shop. There is a smell of coriander and old spices. They argue over what they want to buy. The Indian shopkeeper searches sadly, patiently, among the imported chocolates, the crystalline packets of crisps, for the goods they want. But they are indecisive. Outside the shop there is a huge, revolving plastic ice-cream cone, the beige-brown of the giant wafer battered into a concave shape by curious little fingers. Something about its shape and texture depresses me, it makes me believe somehow that the entire world of pleasure is composed of contrivances.

Next please. *Next* please, says the shopkeeper, beginning to show his impatience.

I had seen her coming in the distance, which gave me time to disappear into the shop with my back towards her. Carmen enters the shop with the Bullfighter. He wants to buy her chocolates. She tells him slyly that she is addicted to them. A particular brand. Don't they sell them here? The shopkeeper becomes obsequious and Carmen, imperious. Everything dwindles around her. The chocolates are bought and carefully wrapped. The Bullfighter pays for them and hands them to her. Her manner is more coy, more coquettish than it was with you, but there is an avaricious smile on her face as she tears the paper from the box and puts a chocolate in his mouth.

She doesn't see me. Or perhaps she pretends not to.

There is a helplessness involved in being a stalker. You have surrendered yourself to them and in some sense you have become the person you are stalking. She is not my prey, I am hers.

They walk out, arms linked, eyes for nobody else. They stop at a flower stall. He buys her roses. White, pink and red, The red ones she throws nonchalantly at the men who made eyes at her, whom she charmed out of coffee houses and cellars, chewing pine kernels, smoking cigars, coming up from the depths of the street, staring at her with their red, slit rat-eyes, whooping like birds. She brought out both the bird and the snake in them. Because her charm has that disdainful element, the Bullfighter doesn't object to her throwing the flowers, even though he had bought them for her, even though the recipients of the sweet-smelling missiles now follow them both down the street in a spell-bound deputation, like children following the Pied Piper.

She has the tranquillity that comes from supreme confidence. She has the power to make you believe she is extraordinarily attractive. I thought of her as a Mayan princess who had to be sacrificed so that plainer, meaner, more mundane things could live. As I follow her I become closer once more to the streets. Although the beggars and amputees and the blind remain, I see a change in the atmosphere of the streets and the army, a leaning towards the people and a growing away from the oligarchy. I am struck with the imminence of danger.

There was a silence and a warning in the air around us all week. Later, I would recall that ominous silence when the events of these times would slowly unfold. The pungent smell of the eucalyptus tree wafts towards me. Something is pulling the universe away from me, like an elastic band, stretching it into places it had never been before.

And yet, to listen to the chatter of the people in the Glass Houses, nothing had changed. They continued to sit there and play poltroon or the tarot as though this was the sole purpose of their existence. Watching them intensified my fear which coiled up against my spine like a serpent. The tinkle of idle laughter in the cafes seemed displaced, like the tinny noises you hear in the summer, when the air is tighter, thinner, noises of radios, children taunting each other, the thump of a ball on the grass. Was I mad or were they?

And I asked myself again - what did I want with Carmen?

The moment when I lapsed into this meditation was the moment when Carmen turned around and faced me.

"Michaela. You have been following me for days. Now what do you want?"

"On the contrary," I replied. "It is you who are following me. You disturb my nights. You send your demons into my dreams and where your witches dance on my canvasses I can no longer paint."

I was dazzled by her strong, dark face, the smile that divided it into light and shade. As she looked up at the Bullfighter, I saw the flash of other lives in this face, the serpentine wisdom of the eternal tormentor.

And I noticed idly the black mole on her calf.

"Yes," she smiled. "But what do you want?"

"It isn't what I want," I told her quietly. "It's what José wants. And what José wants is for the two of you to get back together again." I paused. "I want what is good for José."

"I see," she stayed quiet for a minute. Then she looked up at me. "What happens when the well runs dry? You have to replenish it with fresh water. Stale water will not do. You will become sick from it. Am I right? You, too, would be wise to follow this advice, Michaela," she said before turning away.

❧

At home I watched my mother cursing over her cooking. Most of the servants had left either to equip themselves for the revolution they saw coming, or because the revolutionary ethos had made them realise their place in the world was no longer servile. My mother spent her days fuming at them and trying, hopelessly, to develop the domestic arts which she had always found wanting in them. The work was too much for her. I and my sister took over, and my mother would sit all day in an armchair, kneading her hands.

Now that you had become respectable in the eyes of society, my father wanted to know whether I still wished to marry you. I could see he was concerned to protect his own position in the event that the militias would take the country by ballot box or civil war.

"It's too late for that," I told him curtly. "José is involved with Carmen."

"Nothing's too late," my father breezed. "In this country, while I still have power, many things can be arranged."

How I loved and hated this mixture of wheedling affability and arrogance in him. And how simple it would be if I could say to him, yes, father, do something. Win José back to me.

But when I looked at him I no longer saw my father. He, too, it seemed, was a passing miasma in my life, nothing more.

CHAPTER TWENTY-FOUR

Love Among The Gravestones

I hear the chime of Sunday morning church bells. From the window I can see the fine ladies of the families going to church in their hats and white suits, holding their heads stiffly, walking straight as a bullet. And then I remember that there are no real churches any more, and hardly any priests in the land which vomited them up because of their left-wing tendencies.

Nevertheless I see a church in front of me but there are no bells chiming and no well-dressed ladies walking soberly towards it. How dull the world is when the mystery of prayer, the ordering of the week, is destroyed. I enter the abandoned church and am shocked by the aromatic smell of rotten wood and the futility of old worship. I sit in one of the pews and stare at the altar, I imagine how Jesus Christ must have felt carrying the two wooden beams that became his cross. That is how heavy the silence of the dead church feels.

I long for a safe place. A haven, safety, is what I want now. A womb, a cocoon, somewhere that reminds me of childhood, but preferably not my own, which now seems to me imperfect, confused, stunted by greed. My expensive world is clearly crumbling. I am afraid to go out; I sense what is not yet there, but the political hatred seethes. I tie my hair back and walk, plainly dressed, head down. All the places that were mine now seem alien, all the people so distant, their faces full of elsewhere.

"Think of me as a bridge," said Pedro.

He is tightly woven, in control; if he feels pain or jealousy, I will not see or sense it. He is dry; no grief seeps from him.

Carmen is now working for causes that I have abandoned through the exhaustion of unrequited love. Newspaper photographs show her gathering poor and dirty children towards her.

I decide to go to see her. Iscariot to Jesus. This time as a painter.

Carmen's apartment in the city, courtesy of the Bullfighter, was more magnificent than any of the homes I had seen and grown up with in my youth, and far surpassed my own. She had a swimming pool and artefacts by Mexican artists, antiques, a four-poster bed from Britain, silk-printed curtains and upholstery from France, Italian marble statues in formation along the hall, voodoo charms from Brazil, icons from ancient, plundered churches, filigree silver from Belgium. Yet for all its artistic taste the place had an incestuous narcissism.

I took out my easel and my palettes and all my colours and saw at once that she would be a difficult subject to pin down but I would have to paint her as she was each time, as she felt moved to become.

She sat on the sofa in her satin dressing-gown. I told her that I saw her as a woman determined to live at all costs, totally unself-conscious. There was a pause between us because she remembered our last conversation when I had reminded her of the verdict of the cards, but then she simply made herself more comfortable and asked if I supported her work for the disadvantaged people in our society.

I told her that I thought she had become a self-proclaimed do-gooder. It was always words like that, 'disadvantaged', 'oppressed', or 'downtrodden', or the 'helpless' and the 'homeless', the 'forgotten', the 'disappeared'. Never just names of people. So I asked her if she had ever met any and got to know any of them by herself, instead of just posing for pictures with them and persuading journalists to write hyped-up copy about her work. Years of terrorism and killings, I suggested, had been crowned with respectability. Carmen was now a celebrity armed with a highly-placed political lover and the best apartment in town. But where were her own political aspirations now? Strangled at birth by the statesman lover she called the Bullfighter? The poor were staging sit-ins at banks and public squares, I reminded her, in protest at a multi-million dollar American bail-out package which they believed would only benefit investors and banks, while their own standard of living deteriorated still further. What were she and her lover doing about that? Being photographed in the best restaurants and trendiest night-clubs of Europe and the USA?

Her yellow eyes blazed like a tiger's, and then softened with amusement.

"You want maximum expression for the portrait - is that it? Very well, we can talk about it," she offered. But I became silent. It occurred to me that she had become me, and adopted my life-style in an exaggerated way.

"Do you know where José is now?" I asked her suddenly.

"Yes," she said. "He is waiting. Biding his time."

Beneath the weight of Pedro's body I think of you. Poor Pedro. He smiles down at me. The teeth beneath the lips are clenched together. He is trying hard to be my lover, and not just the bridge he describes. His eyes show affection and tolerance for me. If I don't think of you I can enjoy his body, his flexibility for your tautness, his detachment for your alcoholic abuse. He is the rounding-off lover, the accountant, the one who balances the books.

Today I returned to the streets for the first time in several weeks. I took soup, but it was finished in moments. Impossible to feed these mouths; they become the eyes and ears, too. I went back to the house for more provisions. The street-poverty had not improved, but had become aggressive, politicised by the intensity of media interest which now centred upon it. Everything was different now. And there were political activists carrying step-ladders on which they stood to launch declamatory protests, aware that the ruling party, from whose spies they had previously cringed, were now increasingly helpless.

And nobody saw anyone but themselves.

I tripped over, carrying the heavy pot. I swore as it crashed into thousands of pieces, the residue from the soup, with bits of burnt onions and carrots began to leak onto the road. People knelt down to lick the pavements. I realised that I would have to rally my friends and even my silent sister, Alma – they from their endless coffee mornings, she from her endless musical interludes - and provide a soup kitchen.

It was then that I saw you, lurking, unshaven in a street corner. Your clothes were rags. A red, stained kerchief was around your neck. I remembered the kerchief. You were filthy. We stared at each other for a moment and you didn't even bother to avert your eyes.

I went home and made some more soup which I brought back to you.

"Give it to the poor", you said, roughly.

"You are also the poor," I replied. "Eat."

Grudgingly, you did so, serving yourself from the spoon as I held the pot towards you.

You deliberately avoided my eyes.

As you lowered your head towards the spoon I touched your hair. It was damp and sticky, your face, too, as though mildewed.

"Come home with me. I will look after you," I said, fighting back tears, because I knew it was useless.

You looked up at me slowly. Globules of soup on your

week's growth of beard. The question now seemed purely rhetorical, not deserving of any answer.

"I am living on the streets," you said. "This is my home now. It's the most perfect poetic solution. Don't you agree?"

⁂

On my second visit to paint Carmen I became aware of her voice. It was full, grandiose and hearty. It plunged and soared into light and darkness. She made me aware of how my own sadness had brought a sour grief into my voice. The Bullfighter was affable, but patronising. He had none of your brooding sensuality. They exchanged banal conversation. It was - darling, will you make the coffee or shall I? It's my turn, sweetheart, you'll get coffee stains all over that lovely dress. You sit down and get ready for the painting. No, don't put your hair up, I love it as it is.

The consensual trivia blurred my perception of her as a *femme fatale*. Suddenly I wanted to paint the light and shade of her voice, too. I wanted to be able to paint her searching the cupboards, clucking her tongue, trying to find the coffee. Her movements, usually graceful, were clumsy when she was looking for domestic things she couldn't find. She swore a lot.

"José is on the streets, I told you, didn't I?" I said, as I mixed the colours.

"Yes. And I told you he is waiting."

"For what?"

175

She made no reply to this, so I asked her whether she thought the Bullfighter would be her last lover.

She thought for a moment and then said that she would quite like to see the picture I had painted, and she wouldn't mind if it were abstract or very ugly. She could understand my need to render her ugly.

I told her that she had understood nothing. She was an unconscious being and I admired much about her. I had not come here to hurt her.

"No?" she asked with irony. She turned the painting towards her and spent some time assessing it. It was an abstract in shades of purple. Then she said art would solve all my problems.

"What exactly do you mean by that?" I asked her.

"I mean you could paint your pain and unhappiness."

"I don't want to," I snapped, "because such things, if painted, will come true."

"Then you are a dishonest artist," she replied. "The ones with integrity paint only what they feel."

She added quietly: "You should have painted me dead. That way you would be free."

I found myself blushing with fury.

"Yes. I think you would like to kill me," she replied calmly. She put on her dressing gown and looked at her watch. The Bullfighter had left the flat. "We don't have very much time," she said.

"You and José are two people who have excellent reasons to kill me," she said.. She turned on the TV and sat down to watch it, her feet splayed in her pink slippers which came away at the sides where the fluff had worn down.

She kicked them off. I could see the brown soles of her feet. She began to scratch her toes, complaining that they were itching her; she had athlete's foot because she never dried properly after taking a shower. I imagined her an old woman grown mildly crotchety, oh-dearing all the time. Then she changed her tone again, calling out to the Bullfighter to bring her some ointment for the maddening fungus itch.

"He's gone out," I reminded her.

"You're not in love with him," I observed. She did not reply.

"Is he as good as José?" I asked her.

"No," she said. "But as I keep saying, José's time is over, and I mean over. It's time now to get respectable. That is the role of the Bullfighter. I know you think I want respectability for myself, but actually it is for the cause. José knows - but prefers to moan on and on about being rejected. But these were the terms we agreed before we became lovers."

"You agreed terms?"

"Yes, though I know it must be hard for you to understand. Look around you on the streets. There's still plenty of inequality. But it is different now. It has become emancipated, aware. That's because we have honed our own lives, our emotions and philosophy to the needs of others."

"You have made an art of love in more senses than one," I said drily. "Your use of men is an art in itself."

"That's sex. Don't confuse things. Love is what I sell on the streets."

She flicked the remote control.

"I would like to think that I have had a small part to play in our social history and the politics of our time."

The music began. The languorous rhythms of Bizet's card scene, where Carmen's fate is determined, opened with a fluttering of the fate theme on the woodwind. Softly she began to sing.

En vain pour eviter les reponses amères,

En vain tu mêleras.

Cela ne sert a rien, les cartes sont sinceres

et ne mentiront pas".

With a sad smile she sat down on the milky carpet and shook out a pack of cards.

Mais si tu dois mourir, si le mot redoubtable,

est écrit par le sort.

Recommencé vingt fois la carte impitoyable,

Répétera – la mort.

She sat down, lit a cigarette and waited until the aria

was over. Then she turned the music off and cut the cards. The same message.

"You see - just as the song says - toujours la mort!"

She threw them up in the air and gave a grim laugh. Then she took a strand of my hair and wound it around her finger.

"You should have stayed with us. It might have altered all our fates. José and I might have lived. You would have regained your lover. But you made your choice."

"He *will* live!" I protested.

"My story is nearly ended," she said. "I am ready to go at any time. "

❧

After I finished the painting I went with Carmen to the Place of the Sphinxes. She turned towards me in the dark as the moon slithered in and out of a cloud and illuminated the outline of her face like a mirage, all in silver against the dark. Her hair had the sheer fall of Indian hair. Sheet metal. All weight and no volume.

She waited with that strange and simple sturdiness that she seemed to draw from within her. She was like Hiawatha, listening for a message among the leaves or whispering grass, in the catcall of a predatory beast, in the prowling self that she had become, framed by an austere environment which suited her nature so much better than the abundance of her life with the Bullfighter. It was a strange humanity that seemed to open here in the Place of the Sphinxes, and I saw that

179

she neither willed death nor rejected it. It was the same to her, either way. If she were called by distant gods to another place, I longed to awaken her frailty just one last time before she died. But her face in the delicate, crepuscular light, was hard-smooth as clay.

This was the face that you loved and that had reduced you to a street beggar. I felt a kinship with her because we had shared you: when I looked at her I felt I was within her because you had loved us both. Yet it was then that I remembered my hatred and jealousy.

"Do you miss him? Do you long for him, even now?" I asked her roughly.

"Why should I?" she asked simply.

"He is closer to me than any man will be. He is my killer."

I lay my head on her shoulder. My heart was beating so furiously that I could not catch my breath. I felt I was being pulled into a direction I did not wish to go. Not him, not him, I kept thinking. She remained impassive. I was touched by my first memory of her, the roughness of the calico blouse, the grease mark on the short red skirt, the acanthine temper. She was a poor girl still - despite everything she had acquired. Her poverty and pride, her absurd self-importance and lack of humour aroused a mixture of anger and compassion in me.

Impulsively she held out her hand to me. "Don't you understand that yet? That is his destiny."

"You are wrong!" I whispered. "I can't allow him to kill what he so loves!"

And as the knife flashed to catch the going down of the sun, I thought of the time, the one and only time, I had made love to a woman and I saw the shrinking of her world between the nostrils of the two Sphinxes. After this I must have passed out.

I want you to understand, José, that it's not your fault, nor the fault of the Minister who calls himself the Bullfighter, nor hers, nor mine. We all loved her. She was our country.

Running. I don't know where, does it matter now, just running. Anywhere. Images flash through my mind. The fine ladies of the empty churches. The remembered priest with his swaying censer. *La Bufana* of the Christmas tree, flung this way and that in the trees as the children beat her down to release the sweets that tumble from her, followed in a candle-lit procession by me, my brother and my sister, my little, silent sister, whose hands were always unconsciously reaching for her cello or the piano, even when they weren't there. Snatches of Gregorian chant sounding like the sea breathing. Religious imagery, all of it. The oligarchs did away with it because they hated and feared the priests. The socialists have no need of it. Feeding the poor and uplifting the downhearted is its own religion. When you're a child you don't think about it; it's just one of life's ceremonies like christenings, weddings and funerals. Those people, priests, garbed in serious, flowing clothes, can always tell you the difference between right and wrong. Their faces are always grimacing. Their neutered voices cleaving to the gothic rooftop. Sex is wrong. Murder is always wrong. But even with murder, you can turn it inside out. You can kill if it's war. Or may prevent war.

You can kill if it's the state taking legal revenge.

They can't touch me. I am the Daughter of the Father. I live in a black and white villa on my father's grand estate. The house is neglected because of my mother's apathy, and the servants have all had bad premonitions and left. But at least I can go home.

Running.

CHAPTER TWENTY-FIVE

The Reckoning

I pushed the sheets up over my head. Nothing will happen to me. What did I do? Who will convict me? I am still the Daughter of the Father. No-one will come knocking on my door. And in any case, I had to do it. We must change the story. You loved her. But you can fade out, José. This is my account. I will end it my way. Two women who both loved one man and one country. And we fought, in our own way. A battle of giants. Of two dominant wills. And the female of the species is stronger, I don't care what anyone says.

I hear someone calling out my name. Someone is knocking at my door. Knocking fit to burst. I refuse to open it. I keep my head under the sheets. It feels like there's blood on my hands. Blood. I didn't wash it away.

What's the matter with you? Have you gone crazy, knocking on the door like that? The voice grows quiet, menacing. Open the door. I get up mechanically, obediently, and slowly go towards the door. Ophelia, Lady Macbeth. Madame St Amaranthe, the beauty of the French Revolution, in white, for sex, sleep and death. Meekly to the guillotine.

The knife was in my hands. Poised. She did nothing.

Her eyes did not leave my face. They became like glass. Agate. I don't remember. Mesmerised. And then a tall shadow behind me. Put down the knife. Hard voice. Put it down. Dawning. Coming to my senses. Did I do it? Could I have done it? Running.

Finally I open the door. A vision; a horrible vision. You. Blood on your hands. Your beard, rough and long now. Smeared down your cheeks. All your filthy clothes, your rags. Barefoot. Blood there, too.

You try to reassure me. I will be alright here, Michaela. They won't look for me here. Give me some clothes. You know, you must have some in the big house, your father's clothes. I'll get rid of these. But just a moment.

And you fold yourself together as though to keep the blood, her blood, within you, to retrieve some of the shed blood and let it somehow enter your veins and live again.

What have you done, José? You put your hand gently over my mouth. It wasn't you, you kept saying. I killed her, you said. I was the shadow behind her, I had stalked her for days, you said. Waited outside her apartment. Saw you both come out together. I had the knife in my hands, I said. I saw your shadow. I don't know. I don't know. Did I do that! Did I? I fainted.

It's alright now, Michaela. Stop shaking like that. You passed out with shock. You don't remember anything. I know what you think. You woke up next to her. But you didn't do it. I killed Carmen, not you. It had to be this way. It's all over now. I just need a little help from you, that's all. Just calm down, Michaela. The clothes. Help me to get rid of these. Blood everywhere. I am washing. Washing clothes, washing hands. It feels the way they describe those Holocaust victims, forever washing, washing. Washing of hands. Washing of blood. Better to throw the clothes away. They will never come clean.

I am seeing everything as though through a veil - the clothes, the red water gushing - all our gestures seem to take place with such exaggerated, repetitive slowness. And in the dark. The blood from your jacket is on the sheets. You are lying to protect me. I know you are.

I speak with the same exaggerated calm. The voice seems to come from somebody else, somebody looking down on us both. I am telling you to go. Please just go.

Pedro arrives early next morning. He enters through the window without frightening me, this Romeo. He takes off his clothes quietly, so not to disturb me unduly and approaches my bed like a gentleman. He is so discreet and ironic that I almost expect him to take his hat off and bow graciously to me. Pedro, I must say, was perfect in form and movement but his eyes were quite dead.

"There's blood on the sheets", he said.

"I know. A street accident last night. Absolutely horrific. I tried to save her life, this poor young girl. But she died anyway."

"Spare me the details. You are probably lying, anyway. Go wash yourself."

∂ֆ

You wrote to me from prison.

My dearest Michaela,

Murder was the only way I could get her out of my system. It was not love, I now recognise, but obsession, lust, a desire to possess and finally to destroy. Had she not been unfaithful but merely elusive, the need to do it would have been the same. I had to squeeze her out of my life, wring her out like a wet cloth in order to release that spirit that so invaded me. I can't tell you what a dark cloud has been lifted from me since the act itself.

I speak to you as a Christian, now, although I have so corrupted the sixth commandment. And even before, when I killed the foreman to save my mother. And then you, Michaela, you saved me. All my loves have come from my violence. And they have turned to violate me, darkening my days, these juices of war – I have drowned many times, as you know, in their drink.

What may be right in theory can't always turn out right in practice. To free the land it is sometimes necessary to kill and be killed; every military man, every politician, every statesman knows that. Yet I had no bloodlust, no real taste for violence as some of my comrades had. So how shall a man live?

I see now that my love for you was so much sweeter and older. I am rid of her, no matter what you say. I know that you can never believe this in your heart. For women have a different romantic imagination. The power of death commands love and is its master. My killing Carmen, has not bound me to her eternally. It is not so. I feel totally free of her now.

I won't lie to you. I know you think, because you passed out and suffered some temporary amnesia, that I am just trying to take the blame. But you couldn't have done it. I can only say that through this I am reaching out for you. To be inside your body would be the ultimate homecoming, to touch you in all the places where you came alive for me. To feel you, you, you.

Ask me to say no more. We will not meet again.

Your José.

Your letter exhilarated and disturbed me. I was so impatient, I hardly read the subtext, all that stuff about the initial suffering caused by your killing the foreman. But you were right, then, José, you were right. A hero, a liberator. Fit for the daughter of an oligarch! So we were linked. A joint destiny. You say I didn't kill her. How will I ever know that you aren't just taking the blame for my action? In any case, the knife was in my hands. Explain that! I wielded that knife.

I took your letter to bed with me. I would not part with it. I had fantasies of sneaking into your cell, overpowering the guard, setting you free. You and I would run away together in the night. Both innocent; both guilty.

I smiled, lying in the dark with my eyes open, recreating

this extravagant love affair. The two strands of extreme romance; love and separation; revenge and forgiveness, slipping away into oblivion, forgetfulness.

I didn't know how ill I was when I read your letter. I didn't realise how I was suspending reality and living on some other finer plane. I hugged you close in my imagination, hoping that you felt that hug of reassurance in your cell. All I wanted at that time was to marry you in some private place, and never see you or speak your name again.

Dear José,

After your arrest and your indictment on charges of murder and terrorism, I spent days walking through the mountains and villages. Sometimes mirages appear, both verbal and visual. I hear the call of our ancestors and I see magic cities arising from the hills. I draw and sketch and as I travel, I am assailed by many men. I use the word assail, as opposed to approach. I have become a fugitive. I can't stay at home and watch the relentless pursuit of justice, helpless and alone.

I sit down to dinner with commercial travellers and see the beggar children's eyes at the window. I feed them tortillas. Then I wonder why I do that, and give them the entire meal. Beggars and travellers! They all want to touch me. Love is the only answer to death, they say, and they beg me in the language of fathers and brothers, who want to help me, redeem me, fill the crater in my soul. They sense it, José, in my eyes and in my aura. And unlike the others, my friends, the coffee-drinkers in the Glass Houses, who retreat from it, they approach me.

At this point, if it is a man of means who pursues me, I disappear into the toilet at the back of the restaurant and then out the back way. And if it is a poor man, I humiliate him by paying the bill and sending him off with a fistful of dollars. This is how I punish them. I don't need to feel gratitude.

I sit in cinemas, watching the silent scream of America, the rabid, hurt women, the emasculated, frozen men, the riotous, old-headed children. This sphere of change is coming to me, to my protected aristocracy, to grant me noise and volume and neurosis and the brutal opening of my mind. I ponder the contrast between the two Americas and wonder if there's a point I am missing. And in this distant directive, in this leap from power to impoverishment and back again I see what is missing in my own life, José, my purposeless life, for even with all my art, a life of noblesse oblige and kindly gestures has no imperative. Here I see that the lovers have no love to offer, and the cities no contact.

I think of you as I see the world changing, the democratic New World, so long in coming, drawing nearer. Whatever you may say, José you have helped bring it about.

This is a chaotic letter, José, and it will offer you no comfort and me no answers.

Except that I will never leave you.

Michaela.

At your trial you said:

"Members of the jury, what, may I ask you, is the nature of love? It is the flower that someone casually throws at you whose seed takes root in your heart and grows inside you, filling you with its smell and efflorescence, until you can't breathe. At this point the flower becomes a cancer; one or the other must die, the flower or the one in whose heart it was planted.

"And what is the nature of armed struggle? Armed struggle equally begins with love, with the casual throwing of a flower and equally its seed can grow too big and oppress the one in whom it is planted. Then the recipient understands that the seed is alien, it has no place in his heart because it was planted there without his consent and must eventually destroy him.

"Whether love or armed struggle, liberation is necessary in order to breathe new life. Carmen was my oppressor and my lover. She took me down roads I did not wish to travel. I came to believe in her cause for freedom yet I killed her so that neither she nor her cause would suffocate me."

It was a military tribunal and so there were no women present apart from myself and a few members of the élite families. You had no faith in the legal profession and therefore you conducted your own defence. There was an air of desiccated masculinity amid the shining medals of the top brass, as though they sensed that the days of military power boosting oligarchic supremacy were over.

The prosecutor ranted and wheedled; I saw the heads of the members of the tribunal swivel from side to side as he cajoled them. Their faces were vapid, waiting to be filled with his rhetoric. I saw that the prosecutor had a huge black wart on his cheek. It hardly seemed possible that your life was in these hands - the hands of a man with a black facial wart. The medievalism of the scene oppressed me. They could have come straight out of the "Canterbury Tales", this bunch of eccentrics with their bluff sourness.

I sat alone in the public gallery and began to draw their swivelling heads, the prosecutor with the black wart, and then in your own face I saw the pale oval of surrender. I couldn't draw that.

The trial was a bland ritual having little to do with the original action of the offence. The crime alone had impetus; the members of this tribunal were merely ripples in a stream into which someone has plunged; outer ripples with no internal energy.

My rival was dead, yet she still survived in you. In that pale oval face I saw her, not you. I remembered the smell of ripe roses that her skin exuded, and I remembered its smoothness.

It took the tribunal six days to reach their verdict. We both knew it before they spoke, from the awkward way they stood and in the slight bowing of your head. This small gesture of humility only served to sharpen their teeth, ripen their revenge. Then a shaft of sunlight through the window brought your face into focus and, like a man caught in the arc of a searchlight, you momentarily disappeared. When you returned you had a small, bitter, defensive smile. My heart plunged. Why couldn't I get up and confess – tell them you were innocent! That it was me – I had killed her! Why – why - why ! Then with a shock I noticed that you had a black eye and the side of your cheek was bruised.

This court I knew was vengeful and humourless. But – incredibly - at that moment I wanted laughter. The laughter of forgiveness; the common edge to all our differences. It came to me that when a person is beyond laughter he is truly dead. But crime does not invite humour, only revenge.

The imposing silence of retribution which separated men and which had presaged the civil war of our country was the difference between the empty and the full.

They led you out. I raced down the stairs from the public gallery and pushed past the crowd until I was almost level with you. I could almost touch your hand. Almost. You half turned towards me. But then it was no longer your face, the one I had known and loved.

I walked out slowly into the sunlight. The light that day was particularly sharp, almost blinding. It was late summer, you could already feel the spice in the air, the coming of autumn. I remember being peculiarly aware of everything as though I, myself, no longer existed. I walked through a strange crowd. They appeared to be waiting, hesitant, yet they all looked at me. I almost managed to pass through them. And then this strange silence of waiting. It was only then that I saw the cameras flash, and the journalists all rushed forward as though the sign had been given.

What connection did I have with the killer? As a daughter of one of the ruling families what possible interest could I have in this trial unless I had some secret connection? Did I have some secret assignation, some mystery link with the guerrilla group to which Carmen belonged? Did my father know I was here? Had he changed his colours so late in his career and would he vote with the socialists in the coming election? Would there *be* a coming election? Did I not consider that my actions might undermine state security and bring civil war one step nearer?

I waved off all these questions. As they jostled me all the way to my car I felt a strange peace invade me. I had not dared look either to left or right of me for fear of confronting one of the reporters. Yet I was suddenly aware of a small, bowed figure beside me, wiping away tears. It was your father. I glanced at him and instantly remembered his impenetrable grief when your mother died. It seemed now he would cry for ever. I put my arm around him and led him into the car.

CHAPTER TWENTY-SIX

Acid Rain

I have begun a sort of wake for you. I do not paint and I have taken a vow of silence. Especially I make love in silence. Yes, I take many lovers, one after another, but my salvation lies in never seeing them again.

The silence is liberating. That way they will not touch me. You did violence to our love, José, and in the time of memory and wakefulness I have no pity for you. It is violent to offer love in the silence of night and to withdraw it without hope or reason.

I didn't ask for permanence, José, or marriage. But love broken before its time is amputation, requiring surgery to stop the blood flowing.

That is why I allow them to come to me. One at a time. Hoping to stem the blood. Bind the wound. Become my rival lover.

The foreign press has decamped on the lawn outside the big house. Luckily they haven't seen the studio, which is hidden from their view by trees. Surprisingly they lack the imagination to look for me anywhere else on the estate. But they pry into my life like nasty little ferrets. They knock on the door of the mansion constantly. They phone. They park here with sandwiches and flasks and jump up the moment they see any sign of life in the big house. My father comes out and throws a bucket of water over them. He laughs nastily, and tells them I'm not here and they are wasting their time, but they simply dry themselves down and sit down to wait again.

The journalists don't see the lovers who sneak in to the studio after dark from the side of the house under the shade of the eucalyptus and cypress trees. It thrills me, this secret life, this escape from the media who have effectively placed me under house arrest, and if the lovers come because of the silence and because of the newspapermen, it has given me freedom to feel nothing at all. I chuckle at it. My studio is connected to the big house by an internal corridor. I walk through it into the kitchen to help my mother, and the ghostly smell of the mustard, bourguignon or satay sauces the cook used to prepare still linger, reminding me, as smells do, of safer things, happier days. I watch my father, urged on by Alvarez, the young bull in the field, grow louder, more raucous on the telephone to New York or London, as though the length and volume of the call will bring those places nearer and safer.

I notice lately that he has aged. His ears have that elongated, gnomic look that old people develop and his skin is wrinkled. He seems shrunken. I am still in silence or I would ask him if he has given up hope like my mother, who has packed suitcases which grow dusty on the gritted, neglected marble floors ready for flight. I had never noticed before how the place echoes.

La chusma, the rabble, my father muses, are at the gates. But he has been saying that for months now and only the atmosphere grows a little harsher, filled with the catcalls of the night. Otherwise, apart from the journalists, nothing is happening. Sometimes I see my father polishing his gun as the light falls gracefully upon his silvered head. And sometimes he will swear out loud that it was enough to have one silent daughter; now he has two. Will keeping quiet make things go away?

My sister sits on the floor clutching her cello, eyes vacant. I take her in my arms and remember how she has remained a child. I can reach her now that I am in silence. Once I remember before the terrible dream that took her voice away, she had a name. Alma. But because, after the terror of that never spoken of nightmare, she made music speak for her, we gave up communicating with her in any other way. Now in my head I repeat her name, over and over again as I hold her.

A daughter is what I want. What we want, you and me. If only we had a daughter. Not a son in whom I might be tempted to reinvent you, in whom I could look for a turn of the head, timbre of voice. A daughter in whom I might find an oblique version of myself with you as a mere gesture, a fleeting expression of the hand or eye. It is not good to leave the world like this, José. To leave no trace behind. Even though the act of parenting is the dwindling of all one's completeness.

I leave her like a rag-doll and carefully peer out of the window. I can't stand this invasion any more. It is as though they have peeled off my skin and I am quartered like an orange – falling into slices, ready to be eaten.

They send messages offering large sums of money for

my story. My parents are so angry with me for bringing all this on top of them that the atmosphere at home has become unbearable. I send out a written message to the encamped media that if they will leave my family alone, and give me time, I will seriously consider the question of selling my story.

Meanwhile there is hope of an appeal against the sentence.

CHAPTER TWENTY-SEVEN

La Chusma

Y ou have stopped writing letters to me. In mine to
you – I can at least send them now - I don't speak
of what lies ahead.

Our correspondence peters out. I pray for you and for
myself. Lord I am not worthy. Impure. Diffuse. Guilty
as you. The prayer to spare your life sticks in my throat.
My rationalism, partly engendered by the curtailing of
religion in our country, prevents me from believing it
can happen. Like Claudius, I pray and do not pray. The
only thing that seems true is the ignorance that springs
up like weeds all around me. How could I envisage a
God-in-love when I was prepared to kill – and may
have killed? A God-in-justice may be marginally easier
to conceive, but then one does not pray for justice, one
prays for compassion, for understanding.

So I ask for other things, the power of real intuition,
knowledge, strength to live alone, not to ask too many
questions of others. The power to see you after your
death, yet not with these eyes. I am afraid of the
encounter in the dark. To touch and smell you, but not
with my flesh, because I am unable to understand.

The journalists finally disperse. I resume a semblance
of former life and begin talking again. I provide a soup

198

kitchen for the poor and drink tea with friends. They have a limited knowledge of what transpired between us, and they ceaselessly advise. Their words are stones in my ears.

Months pass. There is a coming to terms. I try to reach you in thought, but still can't write. There is no news of the result of the appeal.

One day I decide I will send you flowers. I hover outside the shop, wavering about what to choose. Roses - the obvious - would be a reminder of her. Perhaps flowers would be too pungent, too poignant, suggesting a life in bloom slipping by. And, anyway, what would I write on the card? What words would suffice, or, rather not suffice but encapsulate, gather you back to me. Make you forget about death? Is that possible? No, I realise the bitter truth that nothing is more alienating than the facing of death; it drives lovers, mothers, fathers, siblings apart. A breath apart. There can be no shared experience of memory. I turn away from the shop.

My father's depression is getting worse. I take him out of the house, the secret back way and drive him into the country, hoping to touch him with an awareness of things beyond the fracas of his daily existence and his turbulent relationship with the heir to his troubled throne – Alvarez.

The extended media presence outside the house, the gathering political storm, the suitcases abandoned in the hall have driven my mother crazy. She has begun looking for some internal solace, and finds it in listening to my sister, Alma, playing the cello. Such things had never interested her before. The clothes she had spent months choosing for her in European spending sprees, now hang lifeless on hangers, or gather dust on the floor. She spends hours on the phone consulting fortune-tellers and tarot-card readers. And so the impending chaos of the world outside their front door have begun to penetrate and destroy the internal fabric of the home.

As I drive my father away, he confesses his indecisiveness to me. Whether to stand in the forthcoming elections which have promised to rout the ruling party he represented, or to disappear, to take the family into exile. I think of you, a bitter fear twisting inside me.

I glance out of the window watching the coffee trees which line the mountains and volcanoes at whose feet the Indians grew cacao, maize and squash. We observe the canopy of volcanic dust inches deep on the roads. We see poor children running through it, dust settling on their socks and dyeing them red. Volcanic children standing in the streams while their mothers beat the clothes against the rocks. As the car passes they stop as they always do, in half-smiling, half-sullen solidarity. This time one of the children picks up a stone and throws it at us.

So many of these children are undernourished, I point out to my father, as he rants and raves, threatening to call in the army to arrest them. Many don't have enough work for the full year. The rural population is as tired as a child in the grip of a virus, exhausted from lack of opportunity, just waiting. Only bad things can enter this chasm, I warn my father.

Why do you defend them? He asks me in a fury. But he

knows. And I also know that the energy which drove my first desire to help them, and whose veracity I now question, is dwindling. I see their angry faces, and while my words try to appease, my heart has frozen.

The wild, hot rains have ceased. It is the coffee, cotton and cane harvest. In the villages vendors sell fruit drinks and *jilote,* the young corn. One family offers us tortillas and re-fried beans. I smile and refuse, knowing these are their last rations, touched that they retain their innate hospitality. Now it is my father's turn to fall grimly silent. *La chusma*, he mutters occasionally, as we turn back to town where the rabble lie in their cardboard boxes, with a vagabond look in their eyes.

"Don't make the mistake of seeing them as rubbish, possessing no soul," I say.

"Soul or not, they will not take this land from me!" shouts my father. "They will never inherit my property, these parasites who lack even the will to stand up and look you in the eye. You'll see. I will fight another day."

CHAPTER TWENTY-EIGHT

The Passing

New Year's eve. The fireworks have begun and will flare until dawn, when the celebrations will turn sour and cover the city in the black smoke of premonition. The people in the rural *cantones* will get drunk on home-brewed *guaro*. They will spill out into the streets and engage in senseless brawls which will end in violence and horrific mutilations. And so the ecstasy of New Year's Eve will bring out all the pain that was suppressed during the previous year. Many will murder their children and their old parents before taking their own lives in a single act of purgative resistance.

I see them as they run through the town in thieving, screaming gangs: they have inherited the will to madness and self-destruction, they are fired by the same spirit of pagan sacrifice as their ancestors, although with less sense of order. Rabid dogs howl down the Avenida Independencia, and behind them come this rabble, *la chusma*, crawling out like rats from behind abandoned churches and courtyards, from behind the rich houses built of black volcanic ash. They come to break into homes, to kill and plunder. But this year, more than any other, the oligarchs will recognise how the hand of socialism wields the despair of the poor.

We build barricades outside our homes, like the *sans-*

culottes of the French Revolution; we run back inside to wait for the pogrom to cease, for the shouts to die away. We try to ignore the terrified beating of our hearts by huddling together, by switching on the TV, hoping to hear soothing words that will tell us that order is restored, that everything is under control. But the soothing words never come.

Instead there is a stream of American advertising, for toothpaste and McDonalds, for politicians with their own brand of hard or soft-sell, for land reformers, family planners, purveyors of instant religion or moral regeneration, or merely sensual gratification. In an instant we have changed roles. Powerless and fearful, we are the beggars now.

Tomorrow the looters will realise what they have done and will spend the day crying and ranting. And then the oligarchs will remember who they are and call out the army. Trucks will roll into the villages, forcing children into conscription. As you were once forced, José.

"You see them," whispers my father as we gaze through the openings in our boarded-up windows." I know you hate and despise them, too. I've watched your face as you stare at them, even when you are handing out food. They disgust you. Don't try to deny it."

The next day my mother bursts into my room, crying. "He's gone! He's gone!" she shouts.

"Who?"

"Your brother, Alvarez! I think they've taken him. He's disappeared!"

"Nonsense, mother. He's probably managed to leave the country. He never thought of anyone but himself."

❧

Your final appeal is rejected.

One day I will visit your family again. They will plough their meadow of rocky soil, your brothers and sisters, poking a stick into the furrow and throwing a seed into it from which maize will rise, while another farmer burns the stalks of the last harvest. With few words and busy hands, they will enact the ancient ritual of the *milpa*, the preparation of the corn field, which predates the Spanish conquest and derives from a belief that because the gods of creation were in each plant, eating the plant was an act of communion.

They will accept your death as they did your life, José, with faith and lassitude.

But I cannot accept.

❧

I would like to say that we achieved the communion of these ancient plant-eaters in our last hours together, that even without touching, we truly lived in those moments, but it was not so. I looked at your face and you were a mirror into our past, because we both knew you were dead even before they killed you. I wanted it to become memory even while I was grasping the dwindling moments of your life - the sardonic cruelty of the guards, the absurdity of the pastor when the church had been all but routed from our society, and the way you had eaten the remains of the sticky fruit from my hands.

None of that matters now. My enduring memory is the first look you ever gave me when we were both children and you touched my cheek and said: "Little girl-soon-to-be-woman." Perhaps it was then that I had seen our future in your face that first day when you came to me like a magician, offering sweets and acorns, pulling your mouth like a clown.

"Little girl-soon-to-be-woman."

And later - much later: "Will you think of me at the moment of your death?"

They gave me permission to take your ashes with me in an urn and scatter them over the valley of your home village. Red they were, like the volcanic dust from which you sprang. Some of the ashes blew into my mouth. The unwanted memory of the rose that Carmen had thrown you came to my mind. I was upset that I had no flowers to bring you. But in my left hand I carried a photograph which I have kept on my dressing table to this very day, which I kiss each night and morning. As I study it your face seems to burst into smile or cloud with sorrow. One day I will tear it up because it has grown closer to my ways than yours. Your true face is delivered up to oblivion.

The village *shamans* used to say of the beloved dead that they enrich us and their passing floods our soul with their light. This means we should not mourn their departure because we have become infused with their essence and it is only the crudescence, the corpulence of the flesh that we miss.

We must learn to spiritualise, they say. But I grow impatient for that concept is still too remote from me. As for kissing, what would the *shamans* say of that? And what of touching?

I did not know the meaning of your loss until many years had passed, until the glaucoma inside my mind lifted and I could perfectly see faces and recall the timbre of voices that had subsided long ago into the seas of the past.

And I can speak of it all, now, without dissolving, without losing control.

CHAPTER TWENTY-NINE

The Escape

Civil war broke out in our country on the day of the General Election. Everyone knew the socialists would win, but just before polling the army came out in force. Still no news of Alvarez.

Huge tanks thundered through the streets, encircling the city with the menace of a flight of black crows presaging death. And so the ecstasy of imminent freedom was devoured by the repressive jaws of the oligarchy.

At dawn that morning my silent sister, Alma, suddenly opened her mouth to speak. It was as though the vibration of her hands flew to her mouth, and the music began pouring out in a shuddering rush of sentences, of forebodings and hitherto unexpressed longings. We who had prayed for the return of her speech now begged her to stop, because the river of terrible words had become a flood. Mainly she voiced her fears over her brother.

And then the world fell into turmoil. Bitter battles between the leftists and the army raged for months. Those like us who had homes, were not safe in them. The little streets where we walked became burnt-out dirt tracks, the windows boarded up, graffiti everywhere. The

Glass House itself, symbol of sybaritic power, toppled and smashed, killing hundreds of people, and became recreated years later as a normal street of shops, in the style of Old Europe. And so the crystalline atmosphere that had enclosed the lucky ones for years was reduced to dust and ashes in order for life to be reworked, built up from the soil and from the labour of a new class of society, the *nouveau pauvre*.

Those who remained in the country became peasants on their own land, discarding their expensive European clothes which fell into the eager hands of the poor, and turning to agronomy and the earth cultures.

Having shed their thick skin, the more adaptable of these families were rewarded by a sixth sense which, driven by an army of earth and ancestor spirits who were clearly grateful for the return of justice, lent them grace and the peace which comes from efficient land management.

But let me tell you now that I and my family were not among those who showed this courage to remain in a fallen dynasty which you and Carmen helped bring down.

Pedro arrived one morning, solemn-faced, bearing cash and a portfolio of papers. They heralded freedom. Not even my father protested. He led his family out into the streets like the doomed Russian royal family, like the powdered aristos of the French Revolution. A leader of a defeated army. And I realised, walking out into the streets, in the midst of hand-to-hand fighting, past the jeers of those who wished us dead, that he had never been a brave man. The multi-million dollar deals, the frenetic telephone calls way into the night were a distant fugue, a bugle call to this defeat, further symbolised by what we decided was my brother's defection to a safer place.

Wearing servants' clothes, we moved like somnambulists out of my father's house, from the secret back way, into the revolution. I joined street criers and militiamen, shouting for justice, for freedom and human rights. I shouted with them in order to merge with the crowds. I no longer cared what I said. I had no gusto for any political salvation. I watched my town and my past slip by into another world. Familiar faces on the street twisted with hatred. Only the acacia tree bloomed on that day, its scent bitter with its reminder of a past that became dream. Everything else was being smashed to pieces.

Alma paused suddenly in the midst of her ravings.

"Our house is being desecrated," she screamed. "Looters have come in. I can hear the crashing of china, the furniture being trampled and torn to pieces. Everything we loved and cherished is being destroyed."

"Nonsense," soothed my father. "They wouldn't dare. We will return soon enough and order will be restored, you'll see. Nothing has happened to our home."

This time nobody believed him. "Come on, shout louder, still louder," I said to my mother. "Or we will never escape to the airport!"

But all of us had caught Alma's vision and could imagine wild animals stampeding in our house, their faeces dried beneath the glass atrium of the hallway, and a herd of poor village women with frightened eyes sitting nursing their babies in our drawing room.

I learned later that this all came true.

The sun bore through the clouds followed by the damp smell of foliage before the deluge.

I feel empty. I go into exile with the calm of a traitor whose fate is sealed. If I am saved it is not through resourcefulness but simple trust. It is not my look of innocence but the omnipresence of Pedro that smooths our paths. Papers, false documents, passports emerge from his portfolio which remains resolutely under his arm as he guides me and my family past the demonstrating crowds. He is calm despite the spitting of gunfire which picks off people at random among us, leaving the demonstrators screaming yet resurgent.

In this, the most real hour of my life, I am asleep while he has been busy. There are helping hands, conciliatory touches, pats on the back. I and my forlorn family are in transit, not just from one place to another, but from a condition. We have ceased to be one of the Families and have become refugees. They have torn up our history.

First walking with the crowds, now running. Running in that daze with false papers, this surreal catching of trains, snatching of a new identity which Pedro gives me. I stare at him as he hands us each our papers, solemnly, quietly offering us new names. Why? I mouth at him. Why?

I almost smile. Why are you smiling, he asks. Because

I imagine myself sitting before a computer screen and rejecting each new identity as it pops up, I say. Who else can I be but Michaela? Michaela to the end of time.

My parents and sister escaped to Europe, living in hiding under an assortment of friendly patronages, a plutocracy here, a right-wing enclave there, always on the move, always needing protection. It was while standing beside my weeping mother at the airport that this inevitability of their destiny struck me as odious, something I couldn't bear. And in that moment, Alma opened her mouth and began to scream again. She turned white and held out her hands to me. I took her hands and cuddled her, shushing her as though she were a fractious baby. I hushed her for her own safety, even though I wanted her to scream on for ever, with joy or with heartache because her voice had come back to her in the terror of these times. My parents stared at her and then at each other. Pain, pleasure and mystery clung to their faces. Gently, my heart floating somewhere else, I kissed Alma and handed her back to my mother. While their backs were turned I knew what I had to do. I took a flight to Switzerland where I had invested the money earned from the sale of my paintings. From there I flew to London. My regret was Alma, but she would be safe now. I had no thought for my despised brother, even thought I could not be sure that he hadn't been killed by the mob. How cruel was that? I asked myself. My own flesh and blood.

The oligarchy crumbled. An uneasy left-right alliance

now rules my old country, suspended between the New World and the New Europe. When I read the newspapers I merely smile. The politics of the past no longer disturbs me. To me it is all the same thing. It is change that gathers momentum and change that puts you back where you were just so many years ago. In charge of change are soldiers in the street, trained for combat, laid-back, dark-spectacled, rifles slung, watching the old, outgoing order slink away like a criminal, frog-marched out of his sleep.

In a way I blamed my parents for sitting on the land that I came to believe belonged to all. I blamed them for their own inflexibility, for their inability to see around corners, and, worse, for destroying your life, José. My escape - my exile - was complete.

CHAPTER THIRTY

Michaela Ageing

I live alone. Almost. Total solitude, I found, did not suit me. I have taken a housekeeper, Celia. She is as English as her name. Her mouth is a prim line when pursed and turns into a wide gash when she laughs.

Celia is sorry for me. In her eyes I am a refugee.

And I am sorry for Celia.

Between us hovers the bitterness of people who have separately known - but never shared – happiness. As for me, I am becoming English. Refined, adapted to emotional disguise. There is also this new, pervasive tiredness. Tea at 4 pm. Sometimes even a nap.

It has been almost 30 years now. With Pedro's help, and some cash we were able to retrieve, I have not been poor. I bought a two-bedroom bungalow in a London suburb. Nothing grand, but I like its simplicity. Celia lives there with me.

Her room is tiny. She fills it with little knick-knacks, porcelain figurines, china souvenirs, dogs or bears, with the name of the place painted in and faded out; they look kitsch and homely, busy with concealment, gathering dust. Since the escape I have developed a mild asthmatic condition and going into Celia's room makes my lungs sing, but she says stuff and nonsense - a little bit of dust did nobody any harm.

The parameters of our relationship have blurred with time. I am the employer, but still the stranger, the one seeking asylum, the one whose life is spent in shadow.

Celia's pale blue eyes are fixed between layers of the past. It makes me think that life inside her is closed, like a coffin. Sometimes I consider asking her to go - I am strong enough now to live alone - I don't really need a housekeeper for such a small place, and she makes me feel old, fragile. But after all this was the woman who rescued me from the gloom, who made me plant flowers in little terracotta pots on the back patio, who talked of seasons, of growing vegetables in a nearby allotment, who showed me how to seize the day in small handfuls, one at a time. She did this without ever speaking of the past or the future.

I spend hours watching and painting in the park where the gardens are drifts of pale greens and velvet greens, broad flowers like a child's plump fingers splayed on the beds. Trees groomed like a woman's hairdo. Everything so orderly.

England.

I found an art gallery which likes my work, and I make a living. I think of the way artists like myself have made everyone else see life second-hand, through painterly eyes. A Vermeer here, a Van Gogh there. And everyday people such as Stanley Spencer painted at Cookham, with bucolic faces of innocent wonder, or veined people you see on the tube, painted by Lucian Freud, so transparent you can see the sun and moon peep through their souls.

England. I could have gone anywhere. But England is for my ageing. I will grow like an eccentric old lady, calling out to the cat in the dark, bending to give it milk, gathering it in from the darkness, pursing my wrinkled lips, old lips I used to admire on elderly women as a child because I thought it elegant; a woman whose lover is forgotten, whose body begins to waver, to lose definition, its blurred outline reluctantly glimpsed in shop windows.

But if I thought I would find tranquillity here, in my adopted home, I was wrong. You will not leave me. Snatches of your songs disturb my sleep. You remind me of the youth I so want to discard. I am restless. Go now, José. You are not wanted. You have become a nightmare - tearing down the curtain which hides me from the past.

And there are lots of places to hide in London. Once I spent half a day just sitting in a coffee bar until I could describe its decor with my eyes closed. It had high-backed wrought iron chairs made to resemble a semi clef and quaver. The walls were hung with peeling posters of current pop stars, all with brooding faces. A waitress with a crew cut and a black shirt sat chatting up the waiter. A damp odour clung to the place and in the toilet there was a graffiti message that read: I am a chrysalis on the wing of a butterfly, while on the other wall someone wrote of her longing to break out of her relationship. Later I went home and painted the entire scene from memory.

But I come from a land where you can move swiftly in and out of dream. The mountains celebrate their seasons. The sea glitters with the spirit of the sun. And the light bends to let in the past.

I don't forget you, José. You are too deep within. Sometimes I see myself walking with your walk, my eyebrows slanting upwards like yours, my head cocked, like yours.

I have reasonable success as an artist, here, painting the scenes of my own crumbled dynasty. And there is Pedro. He accepts that my gratitude to him for saving my life has limits. I will not marry him. I will not live with him. When he phones me his voice is intimate but it does not speak to me. Sometimes his speech is slurred from drinking alone, and these blurred accents against the background of the reggae music he plays remind me uncomfortably of you. They remind me of male weakness and inertia. At least with him our relations are not soiled by love.

I am fascinated and repelled by Pedro. He drifts between sexual innuendo and morbid forgetfulness, moaning on about his tax bills, or about the salesman who cheated him out of a pound that morning.

"Come to me", he cajoles me. "Come to me in a velvet or chiffon dress, or something sensual to the touch. Wear the clothes you used to wear. But with nothing on underneath. Then we will make love all night."

"Take a cold shower, Pedro. Get a life."

When he talks like this I can't bear him. And yet I go

to him. Sometimes in fierce resentment. Sometimes in resignation. Either way, I go. I don't know why.

You said not to think of you as a lover, Pedro, but just a bridge. Well, you know that turned out to be true, he replies. And this makes me feel guilty. Also because sometimes when I come into his flat, Pedro is not playing rock music or reggae, but Michaela's aria from Carmen on the piano. The door is slightly ajar through which the heavy, faded and threadbare curtains billow in a soft late summer breeze.

All of a sudden, as I hear his playing, I think of Alma. I find I am stretching out my arms to hold her – of all of them it is she I miss most. Where is she? A painful and visceral longing for her rises up. I am drawn to Pedro then, because he knew her, he engineered our escape from what would certainly have been a lynch mob, and I cup his face in my hands, his sad, worn, Dalmation face, and begin to caress him. He pulls me towards him and lifts up my jumper to undo my bra. No matter what I am wearing underneath I feel that the bra is dirty or washed out, the straps worn and fibrous, I feel dirty even though he gazes upon me as one does at a shrine. He cups my breasts in his hands as I cup his face in mine, and that is strange, too, making love in a state of compassion without desire. He never reminds me of the debt I owe him. He does not need to.

Unlike me, Pedro has no past. Or if he does, it does not exist between us.

"You dream too much, Michaela," he reproves me. "Ever since we left that country you have been walking between two worlds." And then I grow angry, and all I want is to hurt him.

"I never feel like making love to you, Pedro, sorry, but that is the truth," I say, bluntly. "It always feels dirty."

"Because I am not the man you want, it feels dirty for you, but it makes it all the more exciting for me," he replies.

"But that's disgusting! You should find someone else."

"No," he says. He turns me to face the mirror. "Face reality, stop being such a romantic. Look at yourself. You are ravaged, Michaela, who do you think will want you now? You can cope with me because you can still think of me as a pathway, but not a destination. You began to grow old when José died. With me you can enjoy what you have lost because you don't have to go anywhere. And you have nowhere to go. But what you don't realise is that our sex is better this way. It's dream-free."

I let him rant on as I look into the mirror. I see lines in my face I never saw before. Forget José, I tell myself. My face distorts into yours and returns to me again. Given and taken away. A life for a life. With this ring I thee wed. With this noose I thee hang.

When you are old, Celia once told me, the distant past becomes more real than yesterday or even one hour ago. I refuse to accept that. All is time past. All is dream. The past is just the haze of a half-remembered dream. What you call reality, I tell her - the strong, true voice, the laughter, the physical presence, the scents of love - all these vanish into nothingness. It's all just a matter of time.

My mother turned to me at the airport and spoke the first kind words she had ever said to me. "Don't worry, Michaela, you will love again."

"Lovers yes, mother," I told her. "Love, no."

❧

It is better at Pedro's place. It is only a ten minutes' drive away. I feel freer, there because England – and Celia – disappear, and I am back in a hot, passionate land. When he comes to my house, I am paranoid that she will suddenly burst in on us. It is as though I still need to play secret games, as I did with you, José, in the days when you lived in our house, when everything had to be hidden, even our thoughts.

I love the beige, sallow light in this country. I can never get enough of it to paint. So I take many art breaks, travelling all over the country. Never abroad. On the beach this morning, as I take photographs for a new series of watercolours, I see a middle aged, red-haired man sitting alone, his trousers rolled up to reveal his white legs, his brown sandals, his mottled face cupped in his hands. He has unusually wide-set almond eyes, giving him an air of surprise.

I make my way towards him, to ask if he will model for me, with this bleary seaside town in the background, but something about him stops me in my tracks. Through this lonely figure moulded against the pale, English sky I see my future fading like an old sepia print.

Yes. England is for my ageing.

219

I leave the beach and climb up to the village under a hazy sun. Winding, cobbled streets, shops selling coloured crystals and esoterica, smelling of incense and fish and chips, the pungent sweetness of chopped plywood, men working on scaffolding, calling out to each other, optimistic and regenerative, the close, confiding smell of an old haberdashers shop where the bell tinkles as you open the door and enter an enclosed, womb-like world.

But a grey cloud of premonition hovers over me. The quiet of this English beach evokes something quite different in me. I suddenly remember a print I once saw of an English seaside resort painted by a German-Jewish refugee, but what her work revealed was not the seaside but the buttresses and watchtowers of a concentration camp. Her art could not escape her past, just as my escape disfigures the simple, pastoral beauty I see around me.

I return to the beach and decide, after all, to approach the red-haired man. The idea for a painting, once stirred, will not rest. It is still quite early in the morning. And I will start - before the long, dark shadows, before your feet sink into the sand, before the joggers, before the old man searching for coins with a long rod, before the beach changes consciousness.

I open the conversation. He is not English but American. A writer. I get out my sketchpad and he talks. I am no longer interested in the seascape or the callow sigh of seagulls. I am just listening to him, feeling America in England, the density of John Updike's prose in his language, I am remembering fairy tales, as his voice, his kindly voice drones on, the innocent, drawling America of my personal recollections and the college experiences of my brother.

A good likeness, he tells me. I have drawn a woman eating an apple. In the core is a male foetus with a fully developed male body. On the neck I have drawn his face. Is he being polite? He is clearly bemused.

I throw the pad down on the sand, lying back. I feel him watching me. I close my eyes and see the sharp escarpments of my own country, that irritable, restless red land of jarring geometry. And suddenly I have a wild desire for him, a man who knows nothing of my past, who has no interest in it, just to make love to him and go away. I lightly tousle his red hair, he grasps my hand as I get up, but – no – I can't. I gently shake it off and move away.

A troop of Israeli folk dancers arrive. One, two, three, step, turn and turn again. Clap. They invite participants from the locals. One by one, reluctantly, in their embarrassed English way, the people join in. Turn, clap, turn. All rhythm lost but much laughter. A pity, I feel. I am impatient with clumsiness. I was beginning to enjoy the shift and sway, the staccato beat of these dancers. A blend of desert gestures and Hassidic yearning.

I notice the red-haired man still watching me. His eyes narrow quizzically as he draws on a pipe. Finally he moves over to join me. "What happened?" he asks. I shush him because I want to watch the dancers. "They dance like camels dwarfed by the desert, " he says. "Tightly wound and internal. Could you paint something like that?"

I turn to stare at him. "Are you a choreographer? How come you understand so much about dance?"

"Well – I work in the theatre," he admits.

"My work is a still-life informed by one love," I reply in a mournful tone.

But he is not listening. He is excited by some avant-garde theatre he saw in London, and invites me back to the room he has rented in one of those Edwardian buildings that front the beach. Just to talk, he says. It's not every day you meet a cultured person like yourself. This is a wilderness, here, a cultural wilderness.

Perhaps because of the way I suddenly saw my country when he touched me, the way I never do with Pedro, I agree.

Afterwards we lie together, all conversation spent. His profile is turned to the open window where a young breeze lifts the yew tree outside. A deep and calm sense of pleasure invades me, such as I had not even experienced with you. When he falls asleep I get dressed and quietly leave.

CHAPTER THIRTY-ONE

The Diagnosis

At least I am spared the vision of your growing old. Tamed and sated, like an old circus tiger, you would smell of musk and grow fastidious, like my father, with manicured nails, the half-moons buffed white and shining. My money would have kept you in designer jeans, later in dark suits, a cigar, finally a cardigan.

An old woman inside an old man. When I think of you now, I think of the toothpaste tube, squeezed and folded down neatly to get as much out of it as possible, as my mother had shown me when I was a child. I still laugh and cry about it.

Occasionally a journalist picks his or her way to my home. I don't make it easy for them, but neither do I stop them. I agree to talk about art, nothing else. I say nothing about you. Celia discreetly disappears into the kitchen to make tea. One day, I tell them. But not now. I can say only this. The grey of London has seeped into my soul. The sad years have worked like a weevil, eating me from within, until only a rotten dryness remains. A small, pervasive rain descends, waters the dryness, enters my veins and thins the blood, so that I feel, alternately, dried out and drowned. The reporters look at me with the gentle restraint of the sane towards the mad, but then I close up like a clam and refuse to let them prise me open again.

I find I have to take holidays more often and they do me less good. I catch Pedro staring at me strangely, sometimes; there is barely a flicker of fire between us. Because I am afraid, I keep running. Where to? It hardly matters. Sometimes I can't even remember how I reached the place. At these moments I think of the man on the beach. But I no longer recall his features and I gave him my sketch of him.

In Soho there are untidy lights shooting down from the windows above the sex shops. What secrets, there, I wonder. What could I learn there that a myriad unloved lovers have not taught me? After your death, José, I became a technician, skilled in the arts of love. In this way I tried to exorcise your spirit, succeeded, exceeded you. Now the lights go out. The sex shops, it seems, keep office hours. People emerge in suits, fingering their ties, as though from a business meeting, nodding and whispering. What secrets, what secrets are they keeping from me?

I miss the magic of my homeland, its strange rhythms, the sigh of mountains in the still dawn. I walk. I keep walking despite breathlessness, to know I am alive. The tailored waiter in the restaurant window, hands behind his back - what secrets, what secrets? - glimpsed through the glass in a hotel. And in the gathering dark a car snakes down the black road, its lights, its flashing indicator, merging into the fog.

I must be careful. Missing the land of myth and magic is bad for me. Pedro thinks I'm menopausal. He makes all kind of allusions in order to get me to face it. The European feminists, he says, make such a big thing of the change of life. Becoming invisible is their catchword, he says. Such neurosis, I tell him. No Latin American woman thinks this way. She is proud and knows she is always a woman, oestrogen or not. You've no need to worry, he reassures me. You'll always be beautiful, even when you're old.

Then we are both suddenly silent. I know I am sort of doomed, honeyed, gilded, lit up on the edge of a dream. Or else I am like a train, waiting; and all the people shifting a little, politely, yet nervously, for it to move off. I have noticed odd twinges.

Pedro has felt a tiny lump in my left breast. Neither of us said anything about it. When he first felt it, he arched his fingers around the lump with an air of reverence. He wanted to say something about it, but just coughed and looked away.

The other day I stood in the kitchen and a voice, clear and resonant as a bell called out my name. Twice. I turned around sharply, but there was no-one there. It spoke in an authoritarian baritone pitch. From that day on I felt the presence of that voice in my life, the omnipresence of the Watcher. I was disturbed. I was not free.

I refused to be concerned about the lump in the breast, and rejected Celia's advice to see a doctor. The thought of doctors makes me remember the prison warders. I have never wanted to know the truth, not any kind of truth, since the verdict of the judges in the military court. Celia nagged me, she pestered me with sour looks and grim words as I allowed days to pass, as though I were not even entitled to choose my own time. Yet I don't manage time well. I am afraid. I see the days contracting like the space between the two pyramids where Carmen died. Pedro continues to avoid the subject.

But finally it could not be avoided. I fought the doctors and refused the mastectomy. That - no. Anything but that. And they look at me in amazement - someone who puts death before life. I feel a strange affection for the lump, and inexplicably I think of children.

A child of yours, José! I imagine it - a tiny girl - toddling around the house, her endearing stumble of vowels and movements, her little arms raised at my approach, her crying and her laughing with the ultrasonic thrill that attracts and warns in the kingdom of animals, and then one day it is lost, the knot is severed, and she is almost grown up.

Then I would accompany my sullen teenage daughter shopping and wait helpless while her mood darkens because nothing she can find is right. I would surrender up my own youth to her and grieve for the cub-closeness of mother and baby that passes unnoticed down the years into another state of being. I smile in the tunnel of imagination, and don't hear anything the doctor says.

Where have you been, you haven't been listening, he reproves me. What did you say? I mutter. He speaks of healing tissues, their capacity to rebuild the breast, if I wanted, through a silicone implant. But such vanity in a mature woman! Look here, you're not a young girl on the brink of life. We can, however, give you many years, but no, I said. I prefer it this way. The lump is there for my pruning, for my cutting down. In any case, I prefer to know my time. You could have many years of creative life ahead of you, says the doctor. We can salvage these years, if only you would listen. I had a lover, I reply. He could not choose his time. Let me choose mine.

But I am not so strong. They wear me down. I do a deal with them. No mastectomy but I am prepared to go some of the way. Yet I cannot cope with the chemotherapy. I lie in a daze. I am sick. Most of my hair has gone. The old vanity of the spoiled, rich girl that I thought I had excised, now returns. I visit the hairdresser sometimes as often as twice a day. What shall we do for you? They ask politely, lifting the poor strands between deft, professional fingers. Give it back to me, I implore them. Give me back my blonde hair. My hair which never greyed. I am crying now. And I am ashamed at showing this emotional vanity. Why can't I be strong? They glance at each other. A wig, perhaps? A blonde wig?

No, I am not invisible. They look at me, alright. They see a woman containing the volume of her rage. Pedro visits me, takes me to the theatre. but his poor beaten dog face is so strained now. He is afraid to talk about sex.

And then – out of the blue comes a letter from Alvarez. It seems he is in Spain, having managed to escape through some connection or other. It is only now – so many years later – that he feels free of guilt and is able to write to me! He found my address through the internet. As I read the letter I realised he had not changed. Not a word about our parents or Alma or even me. He asked no questions. I glanced over the letter but didn't bother to finish reading it. I didn't note the address or his email. I tore it up and threw it on the fire, calmly watching the paper curl into blackened fingers and disintegrate. I was watching the disintegration of my own past.

Sometimes I think of the voice I heard. Could it have been yours, José? I struggle in my mind to see your face again. To hear your voice. Impossible to conjure. I think of the photograph of the little girl with laughing, teasing eyes, you once said reminded you of the child I had been when we met.

But I wanted you to see me old, too, containing the dignified grace of my grandmother. Not to be. Pedro and Celia sit beside me, as a I grow stronger, watching TV, reading the papers, calling out comments to each other. The media is full of new methods of sustaining beauty; liposuction, massage, endless diet. Images of American womanhood, with her liberated, muscular body, has stretched our ideas of female beauty, I observe.

"Soon you won't be able to tell the difference between a man and a woman," scoffs Pedro. "I don't agree with it, at all," grumbles Celia. "Now take Marilyn Monroe. Did you know she was a size 16? Today they'd call her fat."

Every day presents another example; a jogger, a stretcher, a karate acolyte, all locked into this perception of their getting-perfect-bodies. I watch. And nothing is fulfilled.

One of your breasts is slightly larger than the other, you once said. I'll call them earth and moon.

CHAPTER THIRTY-TWO

Barricades

I sometimes wake up in the middle of the night. I feel the city solid and monolithic, without magical intentions. Its power is in its stillness at the centre of the storm; you can have faith in it.

I have not been out for weeks now, since the diagnosis, but I can imagine. I make sketches from my imagination but lack the strength to carry out the whole composition. The light is different here. There were things you could do in our world when the light in the winter was still sharp, forming a cold halo from the lifting of the night's skin. Then we would sit together, you and I, in our dressing gowns, our first shyness gone, and touch each other respectfully. At first only this was possible; brief spurts of conversation; the anguish of being too near and too far, terrified and magnetised. Oh - how was it possible that I was so alive then?

This illness has reached me, however, as a great providence, an act of perfect aplomb. Yes, I commend it, applaud it. It is retributive but reassuring. On this we can safely count, put things in the hands of someone else, a higher authority: we need make no decisions.

You took the blame in all things, José. How you judge me now I can never know. Whether or not I am guilty is blurred with forgetfulness, the amnesia that follows too much thinking. I have absorbed you so perfectly into my spirit that I feel our actions were as one - psychically fused, honed together. Perhaps all murderers assume God-like roles, but Carmen's death was an act in which she perfectly colluded.

Celia has been on a mad spending spree. She is nervously filling up the place, barricading it against her own fears. Lately she has begun bottling jams. Heavy jars, yellowing or greening with their contents, take over the kitchen, filled with health-giving liquids. There is a magic mushroom imported from the Middle East which spreads itself across the top of the jar like a thick and wrinkled flower, which she claims to be life-renewing. We must try everything she tells me. She would be better to dust the place, now grimy with neglect, while her coveted garden fills the room with the intense smell of flowers and their imminent demise.

Ridiculous, says Pedro, how you allow her to impose her raggedy old woman's ideas on you.

I am feeling stronger, and with this comes a welcome burst of creative energy. I go back into town with my sketch pad, but then the joy quickly turns to anxiety, fear that I will not capture everything I see, that I will not bring back anything important. I watch the laughing, careless teenagers in the cafes, the evil men lurking, as evil men have always lurked, in the city's dark alleys. Behind the gambling dens, the strip clubs, the cigarette butts stamped and glowing underfoot like a neon warning, I hear Bizet's fate theme from "Carmen", the lachrymose wail of a trombone. Where is it coming from? Is it a restaurant playing a CD? Or is there a recording studio nearby where an orchestra is rehearsing? For some reason I become obsessed with finding the source of the music, but I never do and then it fades away. What is the music telling me?

I find myself in a momentarily secluded spot in the City of London. I see a young guitarist sitting in a doorway where he is clearly spending the night. Imported as I am with all my history to another spot on Earth, I stare at him, knowing that no history is personal and that he is merely another reflection of the homeless beggars I had left behind. I hesitate, then put a £10 note in his hat.

Celia wonders why I make these trips, why I bother to sketch these types, as she calls them, when there are hedgerows and buttercups and all the peace of the country where I could find refuge. Who needs people? she asks me. Or - why don't you go abroad. How long does it take to fly to Florence for instance?

Flight? I shall never take another plane anywhere.

I still remember the journey to the UK. The plane descending and with it that fear that everyone shares but no-one mentions. And all those people speaking a foreign language, like strange birds squalling. The plane, at take-off and landing, plays a tinkling rondo from Haydn or Mozart. "Ladies and gentlemen. We are about to make the descent to London Heathrow. The time in London is 6.45 p.m. The weather is mild with partial sunshine. The captain and crew hope you have enjoyed your flight and look forward to welcoming you on board again soon."

Then the gathering of parcels and bags. Paunches and bellies are revealed as old men stretch upwards with an "uugh" and a sigh. Babies are hushed and rocked by their mothers. A world waiting in a capsule. Hope you enjoyed your flight. Hours ago I was a refugee, needing papers, hustled out of my own home. Now a stranger expected to be grateful. Years of youthful travel helped, of course. Walking past the uniformed men, looking unconcerned as passports are flipped open with only a cursory glance. Questions for me, not an EC national, flying in from a repressive regime, but once they have established I have neither arms nor drugs, I am free to go where I like. And then, walking out into the dim English light, the sudden awareness that from now on I will never see anybody I recognise again. There will be no unexpected meeting - no what are *you* doing here? And then the tube uncoiled like a snake that will take me to Victoria. It smells like a brillo-pad. Tears in my eyes.

Celia flicks on the TV. It takes moments for the screen to warm up, for layers of audio visual technology to generate a glamorous woman on a chat show who says: "I think Sylvester Stallone has smelly armpits." And then the raucous studio laughter prompting Celia to switch channels with a curse.

I think of Pedro's victory. My still wonderful body, he tells me, requires love, attention to detail. His face, as he caresses my breasts, grows pale. I wish I had known you before, I tell him. Before what – or whom? he replies. I think you are what José would have become. Without whom? he asks me. Without you or without Carmen?

CHAPTER THIRTY-THREE

The Bridge

Pedro is actually nervous about sex. But what I don't like about him is this habit of telling me what turns him on. His latest confession was that he likes girls with tiny, bird bodies, cock-assed and with magnificently huge breasts. It brings out all his passion, he confides, it is like seeing a young, helpless girl imprisoned in a body too grown-up for her. Carmen, with her squat Indian body would not have attracted him, I suppose.

"What is it like to die, Celia?" I ask her, as she sits knitting a bed-jacket for me.

"I am not familiar with it," she says abruptly.

"But you are older than me," I persist. "You must have thought about it."

"Why must I have?"

"If I die first I am the one who is older."

She makes no reply.

"What is it like being with a woman who is dying? What effect will it have on you? Will you be sorry?"

"Come on now, you mustn't talk like this. Besides, you are not going to die. The doctors are quite pleased with your progress."

Silence. For once she hasn't got the TV on. I can hear the click of her knitting needles.

"No, but I *am* dying. I am terminally ill, Celia. You must put me in a hospice before I become totally unmanageable. In fact, if you want to leave me now - I should have thought of this, shouldn't I? Why was I so selfish? If you can't handle it, why don't you leave now? You could easily find some other job. Yes, this might be a better idea for you."

Celia puts down her knitting needles and averts her gaze. I see the magnificent prow-like nose. Then she turns to face me squarely.

"I am not leaving. Besides, who would there be to take care of you? You haven't heard of your family for years. Who knows whether your parents are even alive?"

"Well, there's Pedro."

"Well, he's no bloody use. What use is a man at a time like this?"

She takes up her knitting again, the needles flickering for a moment out of step, and I smile at the self-discipline of the English temperament whose rhythms are so different from mine. Celia is without insight but not without self-control.

I decide to alter my will. After all, I have no idea of the whereabouts of my parents now. The only person I think of is my sister, Alma. I will leave most of my paintings and some money to Celia. Yes, I must ring the gallery and discuss all this with them. The rest - what else is there – well, I will set up a trust fund for

Alma and give the rest to Pedro, who helped me, who gave me money at the beginning until I found a gallery which would buy my art. Oh yes, and something to cancer research. After all ...

"One other thing, Celia. You will be my executor. I don't wish to be drugged into a coma just to relieve the pain. I must be lucid to the end. I think I will go out onto the patio now, for the light has improved and I will paint today."

I clean my palette knife and inhale the exuberant spirit of the oil paints. I am alive again and will continue to draw breath and to be at one with the universe. What shall I paint? Everything tangible passes, cannot be commended to infinity. I will paint then, the empty spaces, the vacuum, the blackness of the night and its ruminations. Inconceivable, insulting that the world should continue without me. Besides, how will the breathing stop? Nothing like that can ever stop, I am real, vivid inside my own self. Yet they will draw a curtain around me, shutting out the light, and yes, there will be blackness, descent, descent to stupor, to the final vanity of having the world shrink into my soul.

And was it love, José, or was it obsession? Is there any difference? You see, I must ask this question before the final curtain. I don't have so much time.

The doorbell rings. It's Pedro. Pragmatic though he is, he never loses an opportunity to be with me now. And I notice for the first time that he has shifty eyes. Always moving in jerky rhythms. He lacks your stillness, José. He goes to the pub and comes back reeking of alcohol, stale beer that invades his pores. That does remind me of you in your earlier days. He smells so sour these days. Why is everything so physical? I forgive him because his shiftless eyes come from deep despair. How is it, I wonder, that both my men were alcoholics?

He puts his arm around my waist. For the first time I feel a knuckle of affection for him, almost what a mother might feel for her son. I know that you're afraid, I say. Well, do you fancy it, Michaela. I mean right now? I hesitate, not wishing to hurt him. I don't fancy it and so resist him. Life for me now is a matter of a tide ebbing and flowing. I don't want it, but each time I give in it revives my most bitter memories.

And besides, sex keeps death at bay. It is like King David who thought he could keep the angel of death away by his prayers. Sex and praying. Forgive me if the analogy is offensive. But is it? Are these two opposites, by the nature of their conflict, the nearest we ever get to communion?

He kneels before me. I take his head in my hands, but all I can think of is the damage done to my body: I can't bear lean, arid things, puckered and dying.

And so my own dying flesh repels me. My morbid egoism repels me almost as much. It is as though the magic of my own country has evaded me because I escaped it and came to England. There the dying soul will drift, bordered on each side by the love and certainty of believers.

Here death lies in other borders. Doctors speak of drugs and painkilling measures that turn the soul away. I shouldn't have come here to die because they rob me, these doctors, of the past absolutes I could understand.

But it is undignified to complain. And so I make love with Pedro and for a few moments the abyss is bridged, Pedro is the bridge again, and in the touch of another human I feel the swell of deeper waters beneath. But then the feeling goes. I am left alone again for Pedro is not willing to keep me company and wants nothing from me after sex. This is how he is. He gets dressed and looks at his watch. As he always does. As he always will with the next woman who replaces me. And the next. And so on. A few brief words and he goes. He thinks he is being polite, these few words he says, but he should know I don't care. I want him gone. Wham, bam, thank you, ma'am. What do I care? And that's the worst. It has gone. All my feelings have now gone.

There is a political analysis on TV. The recession, it says, will continue and continue. A never-ending downward spiral.

Tea? asks Celia. Behind her glasses her blue eyes are magnified and give her the look of a walrus. In the slant of the faded beige lampshade, they seem evil, full of intent. Her pale, long-fingered hands do the pouring. So controlled. We watch each other. She pours with endless deliberation. As though there is nothing else left to do. I shall mark out my days with coffee spoons, said T.S. Eliot. Well, alright for him. I am nudged with impatience. She sits down and opens the conversation. It is always the same one.

"Heard from your family recently?"

"My brother wrote me from Spain. My sister, Alma, married someone well-connected in the socialist movement and went to Central America. I heard from her last a few weeks ago. Of my parents I have no news at all."

"And this boy-friend of yours - José, is it?"

"Killed in an ambush by government forces. But we have had this conversation before, Celia. I really don't want to discuss it."

"My memory doesn't serve me well these days. And besides, we led quiet lives in Colchester, where I grew up, No colourful adventures such as you've had. Hard to imagine, really. One thing about the British, you know where you are with them. Now you have so many skeletons in your cupboard. I wonder if you really know who you are?"

"One skeleton, only, Celia. As for who I am, I am who I always was"

"You haven't finished your tea."

"Then you drink it. Unless you are afraid of catching something from me. I think I'll go up now."

CHAPTER THIRTY-FOUR

The Knife

In the studio a late sun cuts a triangle of light onto the canvas. I can hear Celia washing up next door. I imagine her in an apron tied around her powder-blue dress, carefully placing the dishes in the sink. And I remember all her incongruities - the cobwebs above the doorways, the dust gathering in her room. The way she will, nevertheless, roll up a newspaper and frenziedly polish all the glass surfaces she can find.

I think fondly of Celia. I enter the kitchen, wanting to say something to her, something kind, affectionate. The same sunlight that threw its triangular slant on the empty canvas has lighted on her nose, picking out the little mole that she can't help touching.

Was it that, or the light, I wonder. Did it make me see something else, something more enduring, in this ordinary, elderly woman, that I had never seen before in any subject, or any other woman?

"Sit down, Celia," I say. I want to paint you. Yes, now. Just as you are. Forget about brushing your hair and taking off your apron. Just sit down. Please!"

"Oh no, dear, I am far too old and ugly. Who on earth would want a portrait of me? I have no family left. No-one would be remotely interested."

"I want you to become someone for me."

"Well, Pedro, do you like it?"

I submit the painting proudly. But Pedro gasps and takes a step back. "It is her, isn't it?"

"Yes, Pedro. She seems to have come through the canvas while I had an urge to paint Celia. I had never been able to capture her properly before. What do you think - no I mean what do you really think? I mean, looked at superficially, it's Celia, isn't it? She actually considers it a good likeness. But underneath – it's someone else, isn't it?"

"Well," Pedro fingers his moustache and twiddles with the colourful kerchief he always wears around his neck. "Difficult for me to say because I have never actually met her. Carmen."

He says her name - the first time I have heard it spoken aloud in years, and there is a ring to it, an evocation. I sit down opposite the full-length canvas and survey her. I know that I have caught her and I wonder now whether she will lose the power to disturb me again, to inhibit my life as she has done even after her death. The light moves into shadow and I sit motionless. Pedro knows my mood and he quietly departs. There comes a sudden smell of roses, and I see again the white house in all its grandeur that I had left, the arches thrown into extreme relief, black shadowed, and the long quadrangle in which I had played with my friends. Where are they now? Perhaps they, too, had fled into exile. Perhaps they had died in the fighting.

And then the voice I had heard once before came again. "Michaela!"

"Pedro!" I call out. "Did you call?" But I knew he had not. It was not him. My throat tightens. Carmen's eyes in the painting follow me everywhere. I am afraid of hearing the voice again. It seems to pursue me.

I ring the gallery and tell them about the painting. Even though I had intended it for Celia alone. The director comes down and is excited by it. It will fetch a good price. The money will go to Celia, but I feel a stab of guilt at my betrayal. If I have enough energy I will paint her again. And this will be truly, honestly, her own likeness. The director is anxious to stage an exhibition of my work. A retrospective, she says.

A fear seeps through the sudden tiredness that comes over me. A retrospective. It comes to me that this is a spent life, a life already written down. That panics me. I understand Pedro and his quaint silences. The sick at heart often go silent and I realise that my illness has affected him in ways I had not considered. I never allowed him to enter my moods and distant fears.

Last week I was in a taxi driving down the Euston Road and I saw a man sitting by a wall with a hat cocked at an acute angle and a cigarette with ash dripping from his hand. That hand was beautifully poised, shaking off the ash and moving the cigarette up to his mouth as he puffed into the sky. The taxi stopped at the lights and I saw a brief smile at nothing flash over his face, as he sat there. There was something elegant and something vagrant about him.

It was Pedro. I looked away. I felt like a voyeur.

But Pedro has turned irascible with me. He can't handle the uncertainty of my illness. Anxiety has made him impotent. To distract him, he has taken a course in aromatherapy and has found a job in a massage parlour. Perhaps it would help you, he suggests. I protest and yet I go all the same. I lie down and allow him to pummel me. It's amazing how many points of eroticism there are, he tells me, places you have forgotten or never knew existed. His face has the dreamy, filmy expression of a pianist lost in his muse, utterly captivated but strangely sexless.

I praise him rather ironically for his tender, loving care. No other man would bother, I say, and he agrees, who else would bother in this world of men bent on self-satisfaction, self-centred assholes, all of them. His words drone on, becoming a whine. I grow irritated. You sound like a salesman, I tell him. Selling tender, loving care. You and me, we are both impotent. I want to be turned on but I'm totally turned off sex.

We need a diversion, he says, come on. Tell you what, let's drive out and go up in an air balloon. The view will be beautiful. So expensive, I tell him. So what? Just once. Once in a lifetime. You know you're right, I say. Sorry, he mutters. I didn't mean it. Oh yes you did.

We go there laughingly, hand in hand like children. A young man, blond in dark glasses, demonstrates what we have to do. The basket lies on its side and he lights up a massive burner and fires into it as the great balloon billows away on the grass filling up with hot air. There is a resonance in the man's voice and a cool sophistication in his manner. I do not want him to remove his glasses. The nose curves down and meets the narrow line of the upper lip which nevertheless promises fullness, generosity, sexiness, serendipity. He has to shout as the hot air sends a tremor through the circulating air around us. He takes off his glasses. The mystery is gone, but still there is some captivating energy. Soon we are rising over the lush hills, people turn into puppets below, houses and roads sashay away, toy-like and unreal. Everything has slowed down, it seems as though the daily challenges of life no longer exist. In the irony of looking down on ant-people, we turn to each other, our bonhomie grows serious, we feel like the only three people left on the planet.

"It would be sheer heaven," I say, "if only you didn't have to keep shooting fire into the balloon."

"Dear lady," says the blond man, "if I didn't, we wouldn't be up here at all but somewhere down in a heap with the cows," he laughs. I feel silly and girlish again. Pedro asks technical questions. He is a little unsettled by the pilot's charisma. We talk of landing, of the inconvenience of upsetting local farmers by hurtling into their fields. The pilot is sensitive to the animals that he does not wish to disturb in his landing. He tells us of the need to balance fuel levels with discretion to the creatures which inhabit the green fields below. Ironic that his contact with the skies and theirs with the earth should have brought them to this understanding.

At 50ft high he uncorks a bottle of champagne. I shiver slightly. The pilot touches me almost imperceptibly as he pours from the bottle. Here, up in the skies, I remember lying awake at night doubting the future, unable to accept that the present is already past tense because I could not see it as present continuous. Thus the possibility of being catapulted off the earth in a hot air balloon accident or plane crash rarely enters one's mind, while that of moving slowly towards death in a long straight line seems more comprehensible.

I avoid the pilot's eyes. No-one else shall touch me again. Pedro's love has become tainted with self-doubt, with fear. But this man - this pilot? There is an opportunity. Still. A card thrust into my hand with his address and phone number, on which is written - are you married to Pedro? I put it away, blushing like a young girl. What has happened? What has stirred me?

Perhaps, if I keep the card in a safe place and take it out to look at during the night, assessing the handwriting, the slope of his signature, it will almost take on the passion of another relationship for me. Something that will keep me sane and drive me mad at the same time. Being truly alive. This is what I so miss! This is what I had to go up in an air balloon for. To remember the world's colours as they once were when I was in love.

Why didn't you come into my life earlier? I whisper to him as he takes my elbow and helps me out of the basket into which we sank clumsily as we hit the earth.

I toy with my mobile, planning to call him. My hair, although short now, has grown back and looks neat in a well-groomed bob. Call him, I urge myself. It makes me feel like someone embarking on a coy and secretive indiscretion. A tense excitement rises within me. How long since I felt this! I decide to use the landline and dial the number 14I so he can't know who it is. I lift the receiver and hear the deep and sensual irony in the man's voice. I try to say something but nothing comes out. I am in love with the sound of his voice, that's all. I want the voice to continue. But his anticipation fades to impatience and finally, rudeness. Fuck it, he mutters. He bangs down the phone.

❧

"I have to say, that at this moment in time, the cancer has spread," says the doctor.

"What do you mean, at this moment in time? Is there another moment in time when it may not spread?"

"The prognosis is not good, I have to say. However, there is one last chance. You could have an operation, but it's very iffy."

"How iffy?"

"Let me put it this way. Without it, you will have another eight weeks of relative good health, but then the cancer will start to eat into your organs. The way the illness is going, you could literally choke to death."

"How much time did you say?"

The doctor swallows.

"Two good months, and then..."

"And then hell?"

"Well. Not a pleasant way to go."

"But the operation is, you say, iffy."

"Yes, but it's the only chance we've got. It's for you, really, to make the decision. I can only advise."

"The last chance."

"Yes."

"But I could literally die under the knife."

He swallows, moves his pen onto the blotting paper on his desk and begins to doodle. His hand shakes slightly.

"You could put it that way."

"Is there another way to put it?"

It's getting late. I must put out tomorrow's milk order and today's empty bottles. Of course, there will only be Celia. She doesn't drink much milk. Just enough for her cups of tea and her morning cereal. Semi-skimmed, she says. Even she, who pooh poohs everything, has become worried about cholesterol.

I go into hospital tomorrow. So many odd bits and pieces to see to, and of course, I haven't done everything. Still, I mustn't panic. I'll wrap up my paints carefully and put them away in colour order. Then perhaps I'll have time to pop into Marks and Spencer for a new pair of silk pyjamas. They will look good in hospital, those pyjamas, especially if I can get them in the salmon pink I've seen, even though it will only be Celia and Pedro - perhaps not even Pedro - who will visit me, and they've seen me without hair, for God's sake. Then I must make a list for the chemist, a new toothbrush, I think, in one of those new glowing pink colours, I am so fond of colour, and I must bring my Walkman and my panpipe tapes, that will bring back memories. Also Bizet's Carmen overture along with Michaela's aria, it is so understated, that aria, and so important, such fine contours to the music although Carmen gets all the exciting stuff of course, but then she's dead. She died long ago, and I'm still alive. Just. Then perhaps, if I can find it, that Saul Bellow novel I liked so much. Its name escapes me.

And most important of all, this book, this testimony, this truth, that I promised the journalists long ago in return for leaving my family in peace. That way no-one can accuse me of selling my story for cash. Whether I live or die, I have entrusted it all to Celia. Plus the newspaper I have chosen to serialise it.

I'm scared. Perhaps, in the end, there will only be Celia. She has been wonderful, of course, Always there for me. Of course, she gets paid. But she could have got another job, couldn't she? If she'd wanted.

This trickle of pain coursing slowly down my left side. Is it fear? I must not panic. I must be ready. Thou preparest a table before me in the presence of mine enemies. My cup runneth over.

Oh for heaven's sake! Let's get on with it.

And what am I missing? Family? They have all gone

now. Friends and lovers? They all see me in the past tense. A giant telescope trained on the earth from Venus which catches only the light of the past, and nothing else; if he can see me now, this is how José sees me, in my past.

I will miss old age. If the operation doesn't work. The raggedness of age is all too evident. The pain, the swollen joints, the slowing down and narrowing horizons of age. A shrinking landscape.

My mind wanders. I am in the green fields back home, among peasant women harvesting the crops, wearing headscarves against the sun, old at 40, singing gypsy songs.

The doctors merge like trees in the ward. I recognise no-one. Blurred faces. Probably it's the pre-med. This one now, did I see him before, so neat in his striped suit in his office, now got up like a butcher in his green overalls, his head wrapped around yet revealing an incipient baldness.

"Hullo," he says, knowing I wouldn't recognise him otherwise. He pats my toes, pinches my cheek, makes me feel like a young girl again.

"Will it be you, doctor?" I hear myself ask in a detestably limpid voice. But I'm too tired really, too tired to care. My body reaches down to the earth. I have learned to separate body and spirit. You know when you are unchanged, yet people, hospitals treat you otherwise. They only see the body you now possess. They can't imagine any other. A horrible, sour stench rises up from the pit of me. Uggh!

"Can you bring me my Chanel No 5?" I murmur to a nurse. "I can't stand it."

"What can't you stand, lovey?"

"This smell."

"What smell? Come on now, you're going into theatre now, you can't have cologne on, whatever are you thinking of?"

Laughter, giggling all around. She is Irish. Her soft, lilting brogue. This sweet-sour decaying smell of old, sick people who can't help turning to water. What is it? What is it?

"You're imagining it, dearie. You smell like roses."

Like roses.

They are wheeling me out.

"Ready?" the doctor asks the nurse.

She has red fingernails beneath her white plastic gloves. The incongruity of them makes me want to laugh, to make an appropriate joke, a gesture that I am here, I exist; they are the ones who are dead. Even her with the red fingernails, probably glancing at her watch to see how soon she can meet her date.

"Did Arsenal play last night? I've been working all around the clock. What was the score? I take it she's had her pre-med."

Their voices become a drone. Only the white lamp of the ceiling light holds me down as it disappears into a thousand luminous shards, yet returning to form just one. I see a line, like a cardiograph, drawn between my past and present. I sink comfortably into the abyss of destiny. There is no history now. Was there ever one? My house in the old country has been either razed to the ground or transformed into a multi-million pound commercial enterprise financed with American venture capital. Or perhaps the Red Cross has requisitioned it and filled it with doctors like this one, so carefully tending me with his remote, ascetic smile and his mind on Arsenal. Name my price, doctor, how much am I worth today? Pyramid shapes merge behind my eyes. I can see perfectly. I am rising above my body. You take form. You become solid and your smile, oh yes your smile is like an opening in the universe. José, back from the abyss, from the monuments to love and war, smiling and waving.

I go to kiss you. The touch is real. It's okay, you say. A thought-form rises between us like a drift of smoke from an Indian camp fire. At last, I say. At last we are free. But suddenly the drift of smoke becomes a human shape. It moves towards us. Who? The shape looms larger now. A feeling of dread fills me. Gypsy hair in my mouth. That animal smell. That laughter. Bitch, I murmur. You and behind you, her. You. Me. Her. Filling me. Eating me. Carmen. So it is not to be – finally – me and you. It's okay, you repeat. There is room there. Room for all the love. Mea culpa. Mea culpa, I mutter.

"Now." says the doctor. He raises the knife.

About the Author

Gloria Tessler is the author of a biography, "Amelie, the story of Lady Jakobovits, published by Vallentine Mitchell in 1999. Her short stories and poetry have appeared in national magazines and anthologies, such as "Poetry Now!" and "A Woman's Place".

As a journalist she has written for national daily and Sunday newspapers, and worked as an editor and staff writer on the "Jewish Chronicle." She is currently arts correspondent for a monthly refugee journal. Her plays, "The Windmill" and "Unveiling Hagar" have been performed in London.

Gloria lives in London and has two daughters and a son.

Lightning Source UK Ltd.
Milton Keynes UK
UKOW051823181011

180538UK00001B/12/P